T0083535

HALLELUJAH **STATION**

M. RANDAL O'WAIN

Hallelujah
Station

& OTHER
STORIES

AUTUMN
HOUSE PRESS
PITTSBURGH, PA

HALLELUJAH STATION AND OTHER STORIES
An Autumn House Book

ISBN: 978-1-938769-59-7
LCCN: 2020938639

All Autumn House books are printed on acid-free paper and meet the
international standards of permanent books intended for purchase by libraries.

"Autumn House Press" and "Autumn House" are registered trademarks owned by
Autumn House Press, a nonprofit corporation whose mission is the publication and
promotion of poetry and other fine literature.

pennsylvania
COUNCIL ON THE ARTS

Autumn House Press receives state arts funding
support through a grant from the Pennsylvania
Council on the Arts, a state agency funded by the
Commonwealth of Pennsylvania, and the
National Endowment for the Arts, a federal agency.

www.autumnhouse.org

Dedicated to Katherine Min

CONTENTS

Salvation | 5

North of Windell | 31

Shadow Play | 53

Hallelujah Station | 69

Just Like *Blue Velvet* | 85

Rembrandt Behind Windows | 121

Heads Down | 139

Strike Zone | 151

Luz | 171

Acknowledgments | *191*

If some of you have demons in your head who talk to you in profanity or whatever […] don't let your demon keep you off the joy bus.
—Wesley Willis

Hallelujah
Station

SALVATION

SALVATION

SALVATION WAS A casino steamer 150 years before I bought the boat. Small for her kind, built by a private entrepreneur in the mid-nineteenth century when the river was crowded with gambling dens and gunboats anchored nearby. When murmurings of Prohibition made their way down to the lowlands, far below the upstanding citizens on the bluffs, the original proprietor sank *Salvation*, but the insurance company dredged her to the surface and argued foul play. Decade after decade, *Salvation* remained docked alongside a collection of mostly inhabitable houseboats at the marina Hazel bought. Hazel rented to a population that was barred from acquiring fixed leases by way of evictions or criminal records. As for me, I moved onto *Salvation* the year I turned thirty. My mother had died and she left me some cash. I began the slow process of restoring the steamer while also brewing my signature batch of crystal meth, a financial endeavor I'm still padded by twenty years later.

When Hazel called me at three in the morning, mumbling through spirits, I knew something had either happened to *Salvation* or that Lee had resurfaced. But it was hard to believe any other fate had befallen Lee besides death or jail, and I might've forgotten his name altogether if I hadn't driven to the river from the suburbs and met Hazel at the marina.

Lee Wainwright came to us as a thirteen-year-old, and Hazel set him up on the tugboat next to *Salvation* at the edge of the docks where the marina spit out into a swath of backwater on the Mississippi River. Lee had been raised by trouble, and even when struck down by his visions, he was saner than most of the degenerates living at the marina.

As for Hazel, he still owns the marina and works at the bar next to the showers. Hazel is a taciturn man, a failure by all accounts: sued into bankruptcy for corrupt renting practices, divorced, and like most native Memphians, an ex-musician with a single under his belt that Dewey Phillips played on the radio, once, back in 1955. Doctors installed a pacemaker beneath the skin near his left nipple and he irreparably threw his hip out tossing wet clothes from the washer that belonged to his first and only wife on the evening she'd returned to collect her things. Poor Hazel was a man without an ounce of grace; the good lord wanted him to be just where he was and made damn sure Hazel was flicked around and about until he was eventually clear of any endeavor that complicated this design. Hazel was a bartender, a slumlord. I used to be in and out of his bar twenty times a day using the pay phone. Hazel respected the hustle and hated cops, and as long as you tipped him highly and regularly, he'd take down messages and get rid of the pigs. That is, until Lee caught the tug on fire and split the marina; after that, no one got preferential treatment.

Hazel's Bar was always a quiet joint, serving one-dollar Pabst to the residents of fifteen houseboats and their friends on the daily, but rarely to outsiders. Inside was dark and narrow with table lamps in each booth and a boom box below the single row of bottom-shelf booze. He kept no kitsch on the walls, no pool table, no dartboard, nothing that could be stolen. Even the beer cooler was padlocked. No customers ever went outside; they chose the air conditioner instead, but the view from Hazel's balcony was magical.

The backwater horseshoed into the current and the sunlight glittered across the deadly undertow and swirling eddies. Hazel was the only other person who ever seemed to appreciate the view, and that's where I found him after driving from the suburbs to the river at 9 a.m. Hazel was sitting on the deck with an ice bucket full of beer and a jar of pickled pigs' feet.

"Don't make sense what I'm about to tell you." Hazel popped a cap from the bottle with his calloused thumb and passed it to me. "You remember the Indian, from Arkansas. Everybody called him Geronimo, but his name was something—"

"Peter Harrison," I said. "He played mean guitar. We had a band for a while, remember, Banana Men. Everything went to shit when he started working for me—"

"Who cares what you got to say?"

I turned from Hazel then, drank half my beer, feeling the alcohol smooth out my blood. Hazel dug into a hoof, biting at the layer of meat around the bone. He smacked even when he wasn't chewing, greedy for the flavor.

"So, Geronimo comes in," Hazel said, "shows me a photo on his phone, one of them with a computer screen, you know? It was Lee. Not for real but like the graffiti he done around town. This one is painted over with an aquarium."

"A fish tank?"

"It's fresh, Geronimo tells me. Weather ain't even tempered the shine."

"Lee's been dead. Everyone says so."

Hazel handed me a grainy color print, most likely scanned from his office. It was Lee: lean, dark-skinned, with careful eyes, a ten-foot halo around his head—the saint within was always a theme in Lee's art. This likeness had faded with time, nearly disappeared into the brick-and-mortar façade of what, if I were to guess, looked like the back wall of Joe's Liquors. A fish tank, vibrant with color, submerged the Lee from the past. Below, in tiny script, were the words: BINGE IS DEAD / WATER LIVES. Binge had been Lee's graffiti name.

"Binge is dead, see."

"Then who the hell is Water?"

"Some fuck-teen from the suburbs trying to make a name."

"Come with me," Hazel said. He locked the bar and started down the steps to the parking lot. It was unnerving to see Hazel walk. His left leg locked at the hip so he had to swing his whole pelvis out to take a step. I'd seen Hazel move around behind the bar for years, but I'd only seen him move *outside* of the bar once before and that too was for Lee. Even when something went down on one of the boats, a leak, say, or an electrical fire, he'd call in one of his guys to fix it, orchestrating the whole affair from his office. Peter Harrison had revived something long dormant in Hazel, revived him soul and body, and now, he was ready to deliver or to be delivered by fate or destiny. Lee had returned.

We got into Hazel's Pontiac and drove to Main Street, south side, and parked in front of Ernestine's. The bar was closed, like everything else besides The Arcade, full of folks eating breakfast. Hazel still hadn't said a word, keeping me in suspense, but I'd grown bored with the whole thing and questioned why I'd even left the suburbs.

"Come on," Hazel said. "Just over here."

We rounded the side of the building. There was Lee. I remember when he'd thrown this piece up; we were wasted after an Oblivions show and on our walk back to the marina, he'd dropped his backpack, pulled out paint cans, and worked the wall behind Ernestine's. It was my favorite piece because his drunken hand had given this portrait an impressionistic look, like Cézanne's yellow rooftops. What made Hazel's discovery more outrageous than the one Geronimo had found was that this building's brickwork had been painted olive green five years prior. All the tags and gang communiqués were erased, including this portrait of Lee. Someone had to first know it was there and then go through the trouble of stripping the top layer of paint without hurting the graffiti that lay beneath. And then, as it had been with the piece at Joe's Liquors, spend hours painting the blue water, the red and yellow pebbles on the tank floor, goldfish swimming around Binge's eyes and mouth, the silver-and-black trim of the aquarium.

"You know so much, tell me why would anybody go through this trouble but Lee."

"Have you *seen* him? Has anyone actually seen him?"

"No."

It hurt Hazel to say as much. I have to admit, it hurt me a little too. Lee was like a son to the whole marina. He needed that much parenting, you know, or maybe, he burned through us all so fast, he needed that many parents. He couldn't help the way he was, what he saw when he saw things, how he felt when he felt things.

"But that don't mean nothing," Hazel said. "This tells me he's still alive."

"He's gone, Hazel. Even if this is—I mean, look. He won't be the same."

"He could've come back, you know. I would've forgiven him."

But would he have forgiven us, I wondered. We drove back to Hazel's, and even though it was 10 a.m., there were two women banging on the front door and screaming for Hazel to wake his lazy ass up. I left him there and walked down the docks to *Salvation*.

The chimneys had been knocked out long before, but the paddle was still there, seized now, no need to repair the huge wheel because I never intended on charting the water. I'd worked hard to restore the middle balcony and crow's nest, using only filigreed oak from the era. The card tables, roulette wheels, and the mirrors that wrapped around the entire second floor—an open room with a bandstand—were all relatively unharmed when I bought *Salvation*. Some stuff went to the trash, but everything I could clean and keep, I did: sanding the wood to smooth out warps and replacing felt on the poker tables. The roulettes were ceramic and after scrubbing with bleach they glinted like new. I set up a bedroom in the storage closet behind the bar. The loading dock below was eventually closed off and equipped with industrial-style ventilation for my lab, and the crow's nest, once restored with railing and a captain's wheel, was where I usually ate meals or read books or watched the river and thought about formulas and business.

I don't know anyone that lives at the marina now; turn-over is high when 100 percent of renters are transient. I looked to the bend where the backwater reached for the current and found the charred and protruding stern of Lee's tug. I'd been the one to unhitch Lee's boat and kick it off, flames licking too close to *Salvation*, a massive bomb considering the methane and other shit I kept below. I can't remember what Lee called his home, but that fat boat sailed freely from the dock for about fifty feet and the wind agitated the fire and it burned there, smoldering for six straight days until it finally sank ass-up in the water. Until now that had been the end of Lee: a monument slicing the shore-bound waves.

I'd been living on *Salvation*—no outdoor railings, the roof leaked, and everything was covered in mildew—for about a month when Lee showed up. The old man across the inlet woke me mid-afternoon by kicking up so much noise I thought someone was dying. This guy, a twice-convicted bank robber, had thick white hair slicked back with pomade and a devilish goatee, oiled as well. We called him the Colonel.

"Getcha' here, boy. I done told you to stay out the open."

Peter Harrison yelled my name, barely making the words through laughter. I stepped out and saw the Colonel, naked from the waist down, chasing this scrawny boy. The boy was playing the fool, running first down the fire steps of the Colonel's boat and around the cabin before he pushed past the Colonel and ran inside where he stripped and dove into the water. The water soothed whatever demon had presence within him, and he looked around, fear in his eyes, and said: "My fellow Americans, as the 45th President of the United States—" We were only on our 42nd President, a Southerner whose politics mirrored the genteel art of obfuscation, but I'd come to learn that time meant little to Lee and that he *was,* as much as he was anything else, the 45th President of the United States.

"Come here, Mr. President," Peter Harrison said. He was dressed in cutoffs and a sleeveless Cannibal Corpse T-shirt. He did *not* have long hair—"It's like this, man. What if every non-white person acted confused because you don't have a crew cut to match your militaristic ancestry?"

"He's mine until sundown. The deal is square, Geronimo. The deal is dealt."

"Is this a white man deal or an Indian deal, Colonel?"

"As white as me, Geronimo."

"Okay, Colonel. I'll accept your deal. And since it's a white man deal, I'll take the boy from you and erase any debt he might owe in the name of progress. Get your ass up here kid."

Lee climbed aboard Peter Harrison's boat, chattering with cold. The Colonel grumbled but went back inside. I listened to the mumbling and distant voices from within; I heard Peter finger-pick a traditional—"Ain't no more cotton fields back home"—while Lee talked a stream, his voice pitching higher, modulating speed until he was silent and then Peter Harrison stepped out and called to me from across the water: "Sleeping like a baby. Can I keep him, Mommy?"

At sundown, Lee emerged dressed in Peter Harrison's clothes. One by one, the residents of Hazel's Marina—excluding the Colonel—came to greet this celebrity of the docks. He was full of kindness then, a shy boy. He worked to meet the eyes of those who passed through, and as folks brought out beer coolers and half-emptied whiskey bottles, Lee Wainwright asked sheepishly if anyone had food.

"I hate to beg off you folks but all I've had is crackers I stole from that old man. I looked and he had nothing but crackers and bologna but he said I had to wait—"

"Colonel!" Hattie the ex-madam (that's how she introduced herself to anyone—*I run a ho-house for longer'n your pecker known what is*) called the Colonel out of his shanty. "Order this boy a crawdad plate, or I'm calling the cops on your creepy ass."

Head low, the Colonel did as he was told.

I kept my distance from Lee. The other marina folks traded him around like he was a puppy, feeding him and giving him clothes. There were no kids, and I think everyone enjoyed pampering and scolding. I had my own shit to deal with and not just cleaning *Salvation* either. Not much of Mom's life insurance was left. I needed junk on the weekly; my buddy Murphy sold black tar cheap and he delivered. I needed to turn Mom's one-time money into forever-money. I loved Mom immensely; she worked double shifts at two different casinos in Tunica, Mississippi, to put me through college (chemistry), riding her Harley there and back dressed in black leather. I can tell you without hesitation that I bought *Salvation* because of her.

The night Lee showed up at my boat, I was in the process of scripting a formula for *meth-chic* that stole something of opiate-induced euphoria. I had the eerie sensation that I was not alone, that someone was watching me, but this happened frequently back when I shot up. I'd see a shadow and turn to greet whoever was coming at me but rarely found anyone there. This time I looked up from my equations and saw Lee at the window.

"You can come in," I said, my first words to him. "Just don't talk."

Lee smiled, slipped through the gallery doors, and sat as far from me as he could. At this point, the only cleaning I'd done was in the storage room, back of the bar. I'd scrubbed that windowless cubby, painted the walls, put down Mom's Oriental rug, and set up a cot I'd bought from Catholic Mission along with a set of sheets and comforter. No pillow. I never slept with a pillow but always on my stomach with my head tilted to the side. Too many friends choked on vomit while sleeping on their backs. Not me, man. I wanted to live now that Mom's soul had been dispatched somewhere off Highway 55 when a Mustang full of drunk Ole Miss students rammed her bike. This is all to say that *Salvation* was a shithole and Lee sat in one of the filthy booths, the wood mildewed, electric blues and greens, dust besides, and he ran his finger through the mixture. His tongue tight in the corner of his mouth, as if his lips fought to secure the wily thing, his eyes soft with pleasure. He was a boy. I hadn't considered him in this light before, even knowing his age: yet now, I saw his aura clearly, and he was clean. Lee was pure.

I waited, watching him work until he rested. I don't know what I'd expected to see: squiggly lines, a happy sun? Lee had drawn a cartoonish version of me: my eyes holding back suffering with such effort as if my entire face was employed to the task of living.

"I saw inside of you, Sad Man," he said.

There was accuracy in the drawn expression but I didn't feel grief, not really; beyond highs stolen from playing music or shooting up, I felt nothing strongly. Even when I thought about life pre-heroin it had always been the same, as if I was born without cerebral appendages others had in spades. Sure, I found things funny and sad and terrible, but passion—I suppose that's what I'm talking about—I never truly felt passionate over anything, not even Mom's death. But there I was etched into years of mildew and dust and sand, my hair large and unkempt, skin around my chin flabby from the years before heroin when I was fat.

"Thank you, Lee. It's beautiful."

"If you want it, you got to pay. My dealer uptown won't have none for charity."

"It's my table. How you gonna stop me from keeping my own table?"

"I'd give it to you if I could, but this here is money in the bank and Big is money-minded. Just like you over there with your symbols and numbers."

"How about we keep it here, and when Big is ready, he can sell my table too."

Lee liked this solution and he nodded in agreement. "I'll sleep here," he said, "on the bench, so nobody comes for the picture or your table in the night. Thieves everywhere," he said.

"You'll need a blanket. A pillow. I only got enough for me."

"I can sleep anywhere and have slept everywhere, too."

"Where's your home? This isn't a place for a boy."

"Your house is filthy, Sad Man. Where is your people since you're nosey?"

"Dead."

"Let's say mine is dead, too. You look like my brother. Not really. He has some big-ass hair too and them same baggy eyes. I seen you shooting into your toe. He likes the same. I hate feet. Ugly things. Put some shoes on in this house, Sad Man. Until you clean up some. Until I move uptown at least. Got girls uptown. With no feet, just perfect without all that ugly. Put some shoes on, Sad Man. You same as mine but a ghost, not full and dark like him, but white like smoke. We can't be brothers without shoes! Shoes is the bond!"

He shifted just like that: Lee turned over and within him a presence emerged and a long cycle began, a chorus—"Shoes is the bond"—the cadence shifting until he'd settled into a three-four time, like a waltz. His eyes, man, his eyes were terrifyingly clear and hard, and he stared at me with furious whites as if beneath the words, beneath the repetition, he communicated something deeper than rage, something primordial, and perhaps the cadence, the exact intonation again and again—"Shoes is the bond"—was not an outburst but an incantation that kept a truly violent expulsion from taking place. Lee's body tensed, his hands gripping the table, and continued the loop, and I stared, curious and removed until I considered the pure boy within and looked away. This simple gesture towards privacy calmed the demon—there was no other word for Lee's spells—and in a final push, he beat the table with his fist, and my form distorted and the top cracked, fibrous from years of disuse.

Within a matter of seconds, he slept. I never asked about his family, again. I learned that it was better not to bother Lee with questions; there were too many answers inside of him.

When I woke the next morning, Lee was gone. Not just from *Salvation* but he'd left the marina altogether.

We all thought that was the end of Lee Wainwright, even when this big-ass country boy showed up and walked directly to the Colonel's boat. This guy did not hesitate, like he knew the Colonel, or so said Hattie who'd watched the whole thing go down. I was out—who knows where? Most memories were traded in for dope. That night, Hazel's Bar hummed with rumors and theories, every resident present besides the Colonel: Hattie said she "heard the hick yelling up a storm" but Peter Harrison said it was the other way around, that the Colonel was the one upset. Everyone agreed the dispute was over Lee and money owed.

"He's a pimp's fist if I ever known a pimp. Come to collect off the Colonel." Hattie said, nodding around to the folks crowding the bar. "Lee got wily. The Colonel didn't pay."

"But he said, remember, the Colonel said that day: 'He's mine until sundown.' Think about it, Hattie? Would you let a mark fuck one of your girls before paying?" Peter Harrison looked around for someone to back him up. Though I agreed and though Hazel said it made sense to him, the rest liked Hattie's drama more, and so they went wild filling in the gaps of the story. By closing time, most folks had convinced themselves that the Colonel was dead up in his shanty, stabbed or strangled. And after he did not appear the following day or the day after, people swore they smelled rotting flesh. Johannes, a Creole from Slidell, burned candles and some incense and prayed on the dock below the Colonel's boat. No one bothered to check on the old man though. Eventually word traveled through the marina that a bondsman had called Hazel to bail the Colonel out of jail. Hazel had refused.

Less than a week later I walked up to the bar in a celebratory mood because I had finally driven my last load of every rotten, ruined, worthless thing from *Salvation* to the dump. I'd withdrawn one hundred dollars of Mom's money and planned to get as many people drunk as I could before the sum dwindled. I carried a box of CDs and planned to DJ, balancing on that precious edge between nodding out and tequila. Hazel hated when I did this, said he didn't want his bar turned into anybody's goddamn frat house, but he loved when I played Otis Redding and The Shangri-Las and The 13th Floor Elevators. On my way up, I hollered like a town crier—"Shots on me, you bums! Come keep me company." Peter Harrison hopped off his deck playing the harmonica, marching in time, and from there formed a slow parade of folks ready to drink away whatever they couldn't sweat or sleep out during the day.

When I stepped into the bar, there was Lee. He held a backpack full of cheap shit: mechanical pencils, rubber duckies for the tub, votive candles, hard candy. He also had blank CDs and one car stereo. Hazel had crossed his arms and gripped his biceps like he meant to tear away the meat. He caught my eye and nodded towards the boy. The bar was dark, and Lee was moving so fast, talking fast too, grabbing items at random from his bag, and thrusting them into the faces of each resident as they strolled into the bar. He shouted prices: "Ten cents for this pencil. Or a buck for this duck. Buck for a duck. Buck a duck. Big money, y'all. Bring the money. Twenty-five dollars for this stereo."

Peter put down his harmonica, his smiling face rear-ranged; Hattie took Lee in her arms and wept, and he fought her, but she was too strong for him, too fierce. He stopped flailing and let her lift him off the ground. She held him like a baby and not a boy so that his head rested in the crook of her neck, and she petted his hair and when she turned toward the bar, I saw his face in the dim light.

Whoever had beaten Lee before sending him out with that backpack had not meant the boy to survive. Besides his eyes, purpled and crushed into slits, his temples were swollen beyond his ears and one nostril had been cut down the middle so that the single slash now made two infected wounds.

I succumbed, like Hazel and Hattie, to a nuclear rage when I looked at Lee's face, imagining the hands that worked on him, and I tore Lee from Hattie's embrace and sat him firmly on a stool. I could see terror in his eyes, but I could not control my emotions or the level of my voice. I demanded answers. I shook him. He watched me from a distance, his soul gone into hiding, leaving only the husk of a boy.

"Let go, fool," Hazel said. "Bring him over to me, Hattie. Hug him like you done. Tell him this'll hurt worse'an a beating but will heal."

Hazel held a bottle of Everclear in one hand and a sewing needle in the other. I saw then what he meant to do and I yelled "Wait!" I ran back to *Salvation* and dropped three codeine tablets in my hand, broke one in half for Lee. By the time I returned, Lee's face was soaking wet and he smelled strongly of hundred proof and he was hollering, but his entire body was rigid in Hattie's grasp. No one, not a single person, made a sound. Hattie and Hazel moved as one. Hazel doused one cut with Everclear, and Hattie pressed the gauze tightly until Hazel cleaned a different wound and then Hattie's sure hand followed.

"Give him these." I handed Hazel both halves of codeine. "He won't feel a thing."

Hattie dropped the pills into Lee's mouth, held his jaw closed and waited until she saw the boy's throat ingest the painkillers. Hazel did not wait. He threaded a needle, ran the point over a flame until it glowed orange, and sewed Lee's nostril together; Hazel's thick and calloused fingers were confident and kind. Lee passed out before Hazel had finished. Hattie taped gauze over the boy's nose and bandaged the cuts above his eyes.

"Lay him yonder," Hazel told me.

I tucked Lee in Hazel's bed under a wool blanket. I imagined how he must've felt, the codeine slipping through him like warm water, and I wanted him to have more comfort than the pill could offer, something a boy might love. Hazel's room had only the necessities of life: soap, dental-stuff, and a towel. I took the towel and folded it lengthways and then down and over until I held a fat, soft loaf. I raised Lee's hands, cut and scabbed, overlooked in the rush to clean his infected nose, and rested the terrycloth against his body.

Silence had melded with the humidity in the bar and formed a membrane of sorts. I slapped the hundred dollars on the counter and told Hazel to keep tequila and Pabst flowing until the money ran out.

"I'm off duty," he said. Hazel set a full bottle of tequila on the counter and unloaded all the cold brews into ice buckets, restocked the coolers and clicked the padlock closed. "This should serve."

He brought a stout bottle of rum for his own use and neither he nor Hattie looked at anyone as they took a booth nearest the backroom where Lee slept.

I put on The Shaw Singers—"Since He Touched Me"—and poured a well glass full of tequila, grabbed a cold Pabst, and settled into playing music. An hour passed, then two. The solemnness of the crowd shifted into laughter, bickering, and eventually, dancing as the booze took hold. No one, if the snippets of conversation was an accurate test, forgot about Lee, but the lingering sorrow lifted. Not for me. The entire night I kept an eye on Hazel and Hattie. No one bothered the two and so I didn't either. I saw Hazel's jaw working, saw how Hattie whispered at him knowingly and with intent. And perhaps if a boy the same age as Lee hadn't shown up that night, this all would have slid away. Perhaps once Lee's face had healed, Hazel and I would've lived out our lives innocent on Lee's behalf.

No one saw the boy slip through the front door, stealing dregs from beers set aside on the tables. He was there long enough to get drunk before Peter Harrison caught him trying to pick the lock on Hazel's cooler. The kid wore a backpack similar to Lee's, and Peter rummaged through it, pulling out the same cheap plastics. He brought him over to Hattie and Hazel.

"Caught a fish," Peter said. "A scrawny one but there's meat enough, heh?'"

"Why you up to no good, boy?"

"I come for Lee. Big said he tired of waiting."

"No other kid here," Hazel said.

"Big the one who beat that boy?" Hattie asked.

"Sure enough, he did. After he come back and Big learned he run away from that white man. I told Big, all the time I told him, Lee can't run no hustle with all that heat inside him. White men always liking Lee for some reason. Big is money-minded, and money is bond."

"Where Big at," Hazel said, already rising from the booth. He unlocked a cabinet beneath the register. I'd never seen the gun before that night, a twenty-two, snub-nosed. Pretty fucking gun, pure cinema, silver and shine.

The boy didn't respond.

"What they call you?" Hazel asked.

"Big call me Ghost on account of how quiet I—"

"Shut up," Hattie called from the booth. "All y'all. Just shut it."

Lee stood in the doorway, hugging the folded towel to his chest. His face was more swollen than before, irritated by the floss and Everclear but this was a healing kind of swell. He was fuzzy from the painkillers.

Lee did not leave that night, nor would he for years. Hazel had shooed Ghost out, told him to tell Big to come on if he had a problem, brandishing his loaded twenty-two to stamp the point. I had one night of worry, one night when sleep evaded me, and I paced, waiting for gunfire to rain, but that never happened. While Hazel and Hattie sutured Lee's nose, the police had surrounded Big. The SWAT team had already arrested Mother Goose, Uncle Benny, Uncle Boise, and Sisters Mary and Mary and Mary. All stupid code names used so that when it came time, the boys would not know the adults' identities. Big hid for three hours in the abandoned train station; he was sentenced to twenty years. Unfortunately, for Lee, Hazel, and me, he was released in less than four. The night of the arrest made national news, even the BBC picked up the story, but I first heard about the events at home on the marina when the small voices of children echoing over the water brought me to where Lee and Ghost sat on the edge of the tugboat deep in conversation.

"They in the system. Up at Falcon."

"I don't feel lucky, Ghost. I see down from the bluffs, you know, into the river but it's night with no moon so the water is dark. Inside of me, it's like that too."

"Inside of you is more than a river, inside there's also fire and mountains. Big sent you down here as a message to these folks, and you got a doctor's visit free of charge. You ugly for sure, but if they hadn't helped you, then Big wouldn't have told me to come and then we'd both be at Falcon."

"What if the police go out looking?"

"How you think we ended up with Big and his crew, free labor and such? Nobody cares, Lee. You know I got a godmother across the water in Arkansas. She got money, too. She's a professor or something. If I show up, I'm guessing she'll have to take me, right?"

"Might want to wash your ass," Lee said. "Smell like you ain't wiped in weeks."

They wrestled, rolling across the tug, twice coming close to the edge. Neither boy saw me, and I was grateful. There was no doubt that Lee would stay with us, at the marina, but I worried about Ghost, hated to imagine him trekking to West Memphis only to be turned away. Fifteen minutes or so passed and the boys quit handling each other. They high-fived, and Ghost leapt onto the dock, leaving Lee behind to face the water that was at this moment bright and blinding. I caught up with Ghost. Most people would think the idea of hiring a boy to sell meth is a punishable, immoral thing to do, but considering the options, knowing I could help Ghost—not to mention benefit from his underage connections—what choice did I have?

"Listen, kid. Soon I'll need to unload my supply. I'll pay you good money. If things go bad, don't hesitate to page me. To work, understand?"

Ghost took the piece of paper I offered. Nodded and tucked it away in his pocket.

"And Lee?"

"That's different. I don't want him near shit like this, okay?"

"Good, good."

I've thought about his reply—"Good, good"—for years. I assumed he was on the same level as me, you know, Lee-has-got-enough-to-deal-with sort of vibe, but after the way things went down with Big later on, I'm not so sure this wasn't the first seed of resentment sewn between Ghost and me. He was just a boy of thirteen, too; scared and alone, but I did not offer him a paddle to climb away from choppy waters: I told his ass to swim harder.

It took six months to get the lab in order, and by then Ghost had done some fieldwork and brought together a small crew of underage kids. When we met, I noticed immediately that he'd grown, his voice had dropped, and a little patch of wiry hair grew on his chin. Ghost recruited Big's children to deliver the dope. I made business cards that said SALVATION IS AT HAND. I didn't think anyone would suspect a church of cooking and selling meth and I was correct. As I roamed the city like a door-to-door salesman with free dope in an alligator-skin suitcase I found at Catholic Mission. I cooked alone, easier that way. The hard part was lying to everyone about where I had my lab. No one expected me to cook meth directly under where I slept, and it was for this reason that I built my lab on the boat. The hustle, like time, curved upward in a steady arc before descending artfully as an arrow and the meth, Salvation, moved with grace. And the money that came through? I played the stock market with a sum identical to Mom's life insurance payout and only traded when the numbers matched. I kept my meth-cash in a waterproof safe dropped into the river through a trap door below the lab, and when it was time to buy, I handed my financial consultant cash. My portfolio will make you drool, man; let's just say that my late nineties investment in Apple makes caviar look like catfish.

I'm fifty now and I sometimes tell this story differently. I lie to misty-eyed strangers I meet at the casinos in Tunica, Mississippi, where I go most weekends and sit at Mom's poker table; I lie and say that Hazel adopted Lee and that I paid for him to go to a private school and that before he split, he was on his way to becoming the next Van Gogh or some shit. That's not true. The thing about Hazel's Marina is that we were all three-legged dogs down there, barely making it day to day through addiction and poverty; our life-goals had dwindled to one simple request: "Let me have a laugh, man. Please God, don't throw bullshit at me no more, just let me eat some and drink some and die laughing with good company." It wasn't that companionship or compassion took precedence or even came naturally to most; it was all we had left. And so Lee, within a matter of days, was folded into the landscape of Hazel's Marina without much thought about his education or future. We gave him what we could, a home and food and friendship. Anything else he needed, he had to obtain. Don't get me wrong; we spoiled him. Hazel called him up to the bar for dinner every night. When money started rolling in, I bought him clothes, shoes, and spray paint, whatever he'd asked for. Lee's internal possessions came less frequently; maybe once a month some trigger released one of those demons, and Lee would disappear.

Lee took to painting like Ghost took to selling drugs. What Lee could paint from his imagination at thirteen would've been impressive if he were some rich kid raised on art camps, but the fact that he could capture the atmosphere of the docks and the river without ever having had a home or paint before made one believe in genius. By the time Lee was seventeen—six feet and 120 pounds—he had mastered realism and then grown bored with photographic styling. His late work—always self-portraits, always with the halo—intentionally tilted the viewer's equilibrium. The way he captured discordance in his paintings was subtle, so nuanced that at first you were unaware of a shift but as you were drawn into the image it felt as if you were gripped by a psychic vibration. It was only after looking away that you realized you were perhaps sane. I did a lot of dope, man. I'm candid. But this was true for everyone who saw his work, so much so that Hazel told Lee he couldn't practice at the docks.

It just happened that Hazel and me were sitting on the deck looking over the water when Lee, one month shy of turning eighteen, showed up with a giant—seven feet, easily—but there was no gentleness within this man, no light in his eyes. Even though he hugged Lee and tickled Lee's scalp beneath that massive head of hair, even though he laughed and asked questions about the marina and Lee's life, there was no doubting the darkness. You know, I loathe saying this, but the way Lee bounced and giggled like his daddy had returned home might've aided in the choices Hazel and I later made.

"This Big, y'all. My brother. He just stopped by 'cause he said he remembered me coming down here before, thought maybe y'all might know me still."

Big wore a Bulls jersey that barely concealed the nine-millimeter holstered on his hip, new black Levi's, pristine white sneakers, gold necklaces, gold Rolex, and gold teeth. He'd been out of prison long enough for him to start working again and it looked like business was good. I knew two things in this moment: Ghost had sent Big my way and Lee was meant to be his bargaining tool. Big didn't give a shit about Lee, who wore a Dead Moon T-shirt, monochrome Converse, and a messenger bag strapped over one shoulder; Belle and Sebastian playing through his headphones loud enough for me to hear across the deck. His right nostril bulging with scar tissue four years after Big sliced his face.

"Come check out my boat, Big. I've got like fifty cassettes, my own bed, a battery powered TV with a VCR. I rented *Goodfellas* from the library if you want to watch a movie. I could paint you. I paint folks on Beale, make more money than Hazel. Ain't that right Hazel?"

"Shut your ass up," Hazel snapped. The way we were positioned when the two walked onto the deck had placed Hazel to my back and until he spoke, I had not thought about him or what he might do on seeing Big. "Get to your boat. Let us men talk."

"Big come to see me so you can't shoo me off like a boy."

I've been trying to convey what happens to Lee's eyes when he gets hot: It's like all the light and life that makes up a person withdraws and what remains is the cold expanse of a two-way mirror and you know that you are being watched by something that does not want to be seen for it is vicious and too hungry.

"Hey, don't worry, brother. I'll be over in five, and we can watch a movie or whatever."

Without a word, Lee slid down the docks toward his tugboat and battery-powered TV like a sullen teenager. I wanted to turn to Hazel and say "We all gave him that, you know, the chance to pout and stomp off and sulk." But I said nothing, nor did I turn from Big.

"I could drop you both and walk to my car before anyone roused this way."

"Leave Lee out of whatever you got planned, man. Settle with us."

"I don't give a fuck about that crazy motherfucker. I'm after the cook and you know it too. Ghost said you were smart, that you'd guess and I saw too; when you were studying me. It's simple, *Sad Man*. You got Ghost running *my* kids. Your operation is half mine."

Big pulled his shirt up to show the handgun, unclasped from the holster, and I nodded. "What if I tell the cook to stop baking, Big? It's that easy to cut off the supply and then what are you gonna do with a couple of dead men and a crew of pissed off teenagers who, after years of getting paid, are flat broke?"

"Ain't that where Lee comes in? Y'all must love his crazy ass or he wouldn't be here, painting folks on Beale. You can't hide him from me, you know. If we are not square in two days, he's dead. See if I bluff, motherfucker."

"You'll kill Lee if I don't turn over the cook? I'm not going to turn over the cook even after you kill Lee so it's lose-lose, man. Forget about it; whatever your scheme, just forget it."

"This is how it will go. You and your cook stay the same and I take over for Ghost. We split the profits fifty-fifty. It's easy Sad Man."

I understood then. All the pomp, the gold and expensive clothes were a show, an illusion, meant to scare me into thinking that he was on top. The gear, all of it, could've just been borrowed or stolen from some poor sucker. What tipped me off more than his plan, a repeat of the same exploitation game he'd played with foster care years before, was that he'd come alone. There were no bodyguards, no crew. Not even a few boys from the streets.

"You know what, man. I'm tired of the business. I can take you to the cook, to the lab, and we can do fifty-fifty, but I get to retire. I mean you came at the right time. You're tough, right? Know how to keep the kids in line, right?"

This oaf ate my shit sandwich and nearly tapped his goddamn heels. Within minutes, we were driving in Big's sedan to a warehouse I owned upriver. I'd gotten him away from the marina, away from Lee, and Hazel sat in the backseat packing a twenty-two as he had ever since the night he'd stitched up Lee. Big's entire demeanor changed on the drive. He talked freely about his plans for the future—the mansion he'd buy in Cordova and the college girls and parties—and for a moment, I felt sorry for him.

We made mistakes. Hazel only owned one tug and that was Lee's room. We waited for Lee to leave the docks but the depression that took hold of him after Big left the marina without saying goodbye, the anger he expressed towards me and Hazel was deep. I'll never really understand it, the love Lee had for this man. Big must've been kind sometimes. Or, he was simply the first person to take Lee in and treat him somewhat normal. Ghost loved Big too, even if that love was from fear. But Big kicked up a stench—all his giant decomposing muscles and fat and organs—and each day I drove to the warehouse to check on the situation, the smell drifted farther afield until by the time we finally drove Lee's tugboat upriver the telltale reek of death covered the shore.

It was night when we winched Big's sedan from the loading dock and into the shallows. My warehouse was once a distribution plant for river commerce, built around the same time as *Salvation*. With all the windows rolled down and Big buckled in, bloated, pressing against the seatbelt, the car slipped and sank into the water within the hour and then Hazel drove the tug out into the middle of the Mississippi; a taut length of chain was the only visible sign of Big. Hazel released the winch.

Lee was at the marina, waiting outside Hazel's bar when we anchored. He did not speak to us, but pushed me aside, making sure we both saw the hurt in his eyes, and jumped aboard his floating room. Within minutes, we heard the opening scene of *Goodfellas* and saw the blue glow break through cracks in his shanty.

"He'll get over it," Hazel said. "I got over worse things."

I spent the next week closing down the lab, severing all ties to Ghost. At Mom's casino, sometimes, I'll overhear a ragged looking couple reminisce about Salvation and once, when I went to St. Louis for an investment seminar, there was a table of men and women all wearing the same ash-gray business attire, and I heard one guy ask the group if they remembered Salvation. "No? Damn you missed out. That shit would keep you up for days, leave you praying for more." I was a good cook. Mom's one-time money had flipped fifty times over, and my finances were air-tight even then. Why risk arrest? I was only thirty-four, and I could get married (never did), have children (ditto), and do good in the community, like, volunteer on committees or donate to St. Jude (once I wrote a check for half a million to Doctors Without Borders but forgot to sign). If it weren't for how things went down with Lee, I might've gotten out of the game clean.

Where the true Delta begins farther south, where the river breaks and spreads out like veins in the human hand; this was where we figured Big would resurface if the river ever spat him up. We were wrong.

Big and his sedan shimmied inward with the current, a measly looking ripple on the surface, but strong and unpredictable. The undertow, the very thing Hazel and I were banking on to send that car farther south parked the motherfucker a mile downriver from Hazel's Marina, on the Arkansas shore where it's only floodplain for miles. First, the vinyl roof appeared and then the windshield with Big's water-worn corpse facing the western shore. We were lucky in this respect: Arkansas shore meant an Arkansas problem. Big had come to us fully prepared to disappear; the sedan he drove had been wiped clean of identifying serial numbers, the license plate was a fake. And when the coroner studied his teeth, they found a felon who pimped children and forced them to meet a daily quota before giving them food or shelter. Case closed. Good riddance.

Lee saw it differently, I suppose. I don't remember who motored him over to the Arkansas shore when the cops dredged out Big's car, but I'll hex that shit-heel for life because Lee had a front row seat to the resurrection of his missing brother. I was out with a realtor that day, looking at condos in the suburbs with two bedrooms in case Lee wanted to live with me, and so my understanding of the events that followed are ballooned by the gossips along the marina. One of them said that Lee swam all of the way across the Mississippi from Arkansas, and when he rose up on the dock, the tugboat just caught fire. All I know is that when I returned, the tugboat was aflame, and considering the remaining barrels of methane on *Salvation*, I unhitched the tug and pushed Lee's shanty toward the river.

The drama was too perfect, too grand for any marina resident to comprehend the hours it must've taken Lee to paint the pier—THE FIRE NEXT TIME. For months after, safe in my suburban condo, bored and comfortable, I watched the nightly news show footage of a burning house or car or building before it panned to the words THE FIRE NEXT TIME painted in Lee's steady script. I followed the signs. I traveled to the charred sites, pretending to be a writer, but no one had seen Lee, and the cops didn't have a clue about the arsonist. This was always a relief to hear, and the fires, for a month or so, were the only means I had for keeping track of Lee. But then the fires stopped. Until Hazel called me down to the marina and showed me the newly submerged images of Lee, the old portraits—*Binge with a halo of light around his head*—floating among goldfish, I'd considered him jailed or dead.

Still, he was lost to me all the same.

NORTH OF WINDELL

NORTH OF WINDELL

Ruth was allowed a bicycle for Saturday trips to the inconsequential town of Windell, as was every other girl in her school that requested one, but in order to travel north she had to carry the cruiser through a patch of woods and then ride the highway shoulder for four miles. She wore three pairs of wool tights that St. Anne's had provided—all personal items were confiscated at the beginning of term—and two sweaters put on inside out. This, she thought, hid her boarding school status. If any well-meaning citizen saw a student from St. Anne's this far from the grounds, they might grow concerned, even suspicious.

She was now a senior at St. Anne's. Sister Alice woke everyone on her floor at 6:00 a.m. and oversaw the group as they cleaned the bathrooms, hallway, and dormitories before each girl showered and dressed in identical grays and whites. Ruth liked the work. By the time Modern Religion began at 8:00 a.m., she felt fatigued but satisfied by the simple accomplishments of whitening toilets and straightening beds. Her thoughts were quieter then and she anticipated bedtime and sleep as opposed to fearing the long hours spent awake with her mind. No one talked during those morning sessions; they weren't allowed.

Ruth liked this too. She didn't want to complain or gossip with the others.

As far as she knew, none of the students had a clue what happened. She wasn't certain Sister Alice had been informed. But this was hard to believe, of course, because before transferring to St. Anne's, national media outlets had contacted her for comments, and when she refused, they ran the story anyway with information stolen from other news outlets that had reported ill-informed facts. Her name and face had been in the local paper next to Max's—they'd used a photo of the couple at the Mid-South Fair. He was wearing a black hoodie and Yankees cap tipped to the side, and while she wore her daily wardrobe—Copout T-shirt with the collar excised and tight jeans—she'd recently shaved her head. She hadn't liked the buzz cut. It had been Max's idea. Though she looked happy in the photograph, she recalled that her smile was a reflection of how pleased he had been by the move. "My girl is fucking hard," he'd told his bandmate, Scotty.

Her hair was long now, nearly down to her shoulders and auburn as opposed to dyed black. She'd gained weight since coming to St. Anne's, almost twenty pounds, and she was allowed to go by her middle name, Elizabeth, instead of Ruth.

Through the first two miles of riding the ancient single-speed, she felt an inner-laughter earned through defiance. This transgression reminded her of who she had been: a public-school junior who smoked weed and hung out with a few friends, and for a time, Max, her first boyfriend and inheritor of her big V. That's how she imagined it, not as an act of carnality, not like Max must've felt as he shook all over, but as ceremony. She kept some of the blood that flowed later, dried now on a white shirt and preserved in a sandwich bag in her dresser back home.

By the fourth and final mile, fear seeped from her pores until her sweat smelled of rotten mushrooms. Every car that passed she believed would be a Sister. She counted the dividing yellow lines, stopping and starting again every time the dashes connected into a double-thread. The speed with which she rode provided a slow count so that by the time she'd reached two, her mind had forgotten about one. In this way, she distracted herself from every impulse to turn around.

After the trial, Ruth's mother paid for a high-end psychiatrist who Ruth visited twice a week: Monday and Friday. She liked Dr. Rushani, whose face had no nuance: her lips were so thin they appeared nonexistent, she had large blue eyes but invisible eyelashes, and her tall frame was without curves or fat. She had a withdrawn disposition that could be easily mistaken for coldness.

Ruth had not told Dr. Rushani about her previous visit to the Mexican restaurant north of Windell. Dr. Rushani often talked of moving on in a way that barely hid her disgust for Ruth's lingering attachment to Max.

"First love is the hardest," Dr. Rushani often said when they were getting to know one another. "But you are stronger than this infatuation. It'll take time, Ruth. There is so much more to come after this moment. You are young and pretty."

"Do you know how many views the recent upload has? Last Saturday it was almost one million."

Dr. Rushani reddened and it seemed she worked harder to hold Ruth's gaze. Ruth knew then Dr. Rushani had watched the video. No matter how many lawyers and business agents her parents communicated with there was always someone who had captured the video in a private file and happily uploaded it again with a new name as soon as one site took it down.

Ruth had not met Max at high school but at a punk show in the basement below a coffee shop near the university. He was five years older, twenty-one to her sixteen, and had a beard that only covered his neckline while the rest of his face was clean-shaven. His fingers and hands were tattooed with skeleton bones, and his hair was long and large and had been bleached orange-yellow. He wore filthy jeans and a Taintskins T-shirt torn at the collar and smelled of soil and sweat and garlic. Ruth had gone to the show with her little brother, Pat, but left with Max. While one band broke down musical equipment and Max's band set up drums and speaker cabinets, he approached her and said, "There is no one else I'd rather crawl into bed naked with. Am I a creep for saying that to you?"

"Yes," she said.

But she waited, watched as he yelled into the microphone, his voice strangely high and whiney. He sounded bored, as if performing was like standing in line at the DMV. She waited until he loaded equipment into a white van, waited while he talked to nearly every person at the club, joined him silently in the backseat of an El Dorado and smoked a joint, shared his pint of Jack, and then climbed onto the seat of his bicycle and rode to his house. She undressed when he asked her to before getting into bed. They did not have sex that night; he said he didn't want to take anyone's virginity. Too much responsibility, he said. Too much commitment.

"Go down on me instead," he said. And she did. She wanted (though this was Ruth's first time) him to yell when he came, the way men did in amateur videos she loved to watch on YouPorn.

"Now you go down on me," she said.

Pat refused to cover for Ruth when she stayed over at Max's house, and so Max often snuck in through the basement window of her childhood room. He didn't like it there, but he wanted her. She painted the walls maroon and tacked up photocopied fliers and posters, bought seven inches and listened to music at full volume to keep him through the night. He always split after hooking up. "It's just too weird, like, I have to think about how young you are, about your parents and little brother."

"I'm sixteen. Not a child."

"I could go to jail. All it takes is one pissed-off father."

It turned out that neither parent really cared about Max's age or that their daughter began spending more time away from home. She had no intention of going to college, hadn't even applied.

They acted as if she would soon be someone else's problem, someone else's baby girl maybe with her own baby girl. So why worry over minor legalities? They did not like Max, however. Every time Max left, her mother vacuumed and then lit candles and laundered Ruth's bedding, trying to rid the house of his pungency. Her father sneered and shook his head any time Max offered his hand for hello. Soon, Ruth had moved in with Max. She took public transportation to school from his neighborhood in the morning and then caught a ride back with friends who needed a safe place to get stoned.

Her seventeenth birthday came towards the end of fall semester in November, and her father gifted her his old video camera. She made stop-start animations of her stuffed animals walking across her pink comforter and then began documenting the bus and the halls at school and the car rides and Max's room.

"Tell me about the video. How did it come about?"

"What do you mean? It was one of many."

"But this one in particular. What was the, I don't know, impetus behind—"

"We never, like, scripted anything. What was recorded was just what we were doing."

Dr. Rushani, who normally sat in a villainously tall chair, stepped around her desk. Rain spat against the unadorned window. Ruth sank deeper into the leather sofa as Dr. Rushani approached. She used to mock the psych-office motif, with the deep desk, clean but for an elephant idol carved from ivory (a cruel lesson, Ruth thought, in the limits of compassion) and books in neat rows, but soon she came to appreciate the room. She was allowed distance beyond time and space, a treat compared to her now uncertain future and present. This was disrupted, however, when Dr. Rushani abandoned her perch, placed her hand on Ruth's forearm, and called her brave.

"I've seen him, you know, since the restraining order." She had not planned on telling Dr. Rushani about seeing Max, but her touch and the word brave and the proximity made Ruth want to hurt Dr. Rushani. She wanted to collapse Dr. Rushani's role, to make her question any sense of control she might believe she held over the situation. There were other ways Ruth could have elicited the facial contortions Dr. Rushani cycled through before backing away, a simple turning of perceived truths perhaps. Dr. Rushani was a professional, and beyond initial shock (and revulsion, if Ruth read her expression correctly), she casually shifted her attentions to the Mexican restaurant.

"I suppose it makes sense to want to see him. The immediate separation must've been stunning for you both. But, you know, he could get into a lot of trouble were anyone to report your visit."

"You threatening to tell?"

"If calling your mother would convince you to stay away from this man, a man I believe to be highly manipulative, then perhaps. You are a minor and part of my job is to say when I feel you are acting unsafe. I do not think it would work nor do I think a total moratorium on all things Max is reasonable or healthy. So, no, I'm not threatening you. I'd rather you talk it out with me before you turn inward, or worse, take your heartbreak out on yourself. Let's start with an easy question: How did you find him?"

"It's pretty hilarious, actually. Through my mother."

The first month of spring semester at St. Anne's, Ruth's mother took her shopping, and afterwards, they ate lunch at Tacos Jalisco. Max, wearing a red apron and Vans with duct tape across the toe to keep the sole from flapping, walked out of the kitchen with a tray of clean plates and stacked them behind the bar. Ruth hid from him then, not willing to see what her face, her being, looked like reflected in his surprised expression. She feigned sudden and fierce cramps and laid down in the booth, complaining until her mother drove her to St. Anne's without eating.

A week later, she rode her bike to see him.

"I knew, were you to locate him, you'd do something rash. Would he seek you out were he to know where you were?"

Dr. Rushani would not have condoned a meeting between the couple in the beginning. Months ago, she would've remained firm, but cautious. To Ruth, it was still obvious that indignation guided Dr. Rushani's counsel; she saw a teenage girl who'd been a victim of a grave and humiliating experience. Max was the perpetrator, and Dr. Rushani guided all mention of him away from the light. It was for the best, Ruth thought. Everyone—from her mother and father to the police to lawyers to her friends to Dr. Rushani—wanted her to be a victim, and under the glare of such consistent fury and judgment, she quickly accepted the role. Now she saw that Dr. Rushani, however misinformed, wanted to understand Ruth.

"How did you feel seeing him? I know that sounds stupid to you, but I'd like to know—good or bad?"

"He looked terrible, like his spirit had been stolen."

"Jail is rumored to do that to some people, but not permanently."

"How would you know anything about jail?"

"I don't. But I'm divorced—" Ruth must've smiled at this breach of professionalism because Dr. Rushani did not continue. "Just describe the meeting. Was he surprised?"

"He was hurt more than angry."

Ruth had parked her bike and went in through the kitchen door. A kitchen was a kitchen was a kitchen, and she found the dish pit easily. She nearly threw herself to the floor from exhaustion and disappointment when she saw that Max was not at the station: dishes stacked high, a half-full glass rack. There was no one around. She turned in a circle, noticing the bean and meat spattered stovetops, a liquid current moving bits of tortilla around the fry vat. Ranchera played from a small radio. Ruth peeked through the server doors and saw Max sitting with the cooks beneath TVs playing football. She watched him for what felt like minutes, the seams in the armpit of his red T-shirt had ripped, and she could see the tattoo of an owl that covered his side. He'd shaved his head and beard and wore a knit cap. This change made him look small. Ruth still felt a touch-memory of holding tight to his hair and wanted to weep at this loss, a loss that seemed more unjust than any other punishment. It was then that Max caught sight of her behind the waiter doors. He slyly shifted his gaze behind where Ruth stood and spoke loudly when he said that he was going out back to smoke.

Ruth stood near her bike and waited until Max rounded the corner of the building from the front. He didn't turn or acknowledge her at all, but crossed behind the dumpsters and disappeared. Ruth found him sitting on top of a walk-in freezer abandoned in the thick of tall grass. He was rolling a cigarette, and even when he licked the glue, he did not make eye contact with Ruth.

"Stay down there," he'd said. "I don't want you up here. I'm visible to anyone driving by, but no one can see you. Why are you fucking with me, Ruth? I'm trying. I can't go back to jail, not even for a couple months."

Ruth didn't speak. With her brother and her friends from school, she had a reputation for talking too much, too loudly. Pat used to put his hand up to block her face each morning before she had the chance to tell him about a dream, her weekend plans, or homework. With Max, she rarely spoke, and he'd come to think of her as a quiet person. She watched him up there, the winter reddening his fingers. Wind picked at her cheeks like paper cuts. As if he had known she would ask, he told her he'd shaved his head before going to jail so that it could not be used against him in a fight.

Whether from the bike ride or from the image of faceless men holding Max by the hair and beating him in a cellblock she could only imagine as a TV scene, bile arose in the back of her mouth, and she vomited into the grass. He jumped down and held her hair as she heaved orange juice and oatmeal. She rested against his body. She did not want to see his eyes, dim and serious, so different from the laughing Max she'd loved. With great effort, she pulled away from his body and looked into his face, the face of a man who knew he was no longer free to be reckless.

She had not told Dr. Rushani this realization; it would have brought her dangerously close to the edges of truth. And Dr. Rushani might have dismissed his demeanor as being one of fear. He was not afraid and Ruth knew this. Max was lost, not just to her, but to himself as well.

It went like this: they made out nightly, naked, for a month before Max began to ask. If he had ever questioned her reasons for waiting, she would've been at a loss to explain. She was bothered by the rearrangement of her body; the subtraction instead of addition freaked her out. If sex marked you externally, if the first time was tattooed, say, this would have been easier for her. She'd never handled lasts very well. As a child, she cried on Christmas when there were no more presents left to open, cried before she began to peel back the layers of the first gift, her father tensing in his recliner, wordless, while her mother said again and again, "Open your present. Open your present, Ruth. Open your present. Ruth. Open—" And when she finally gave in, it was not because Max had tensed or demanded for her to open, no, that would at least have cinematic precedent. He whined and rolled over to face the wall.

They had been making out for hours but without joy. Max moved his hips, his mind lost to bodily need, so that every few seconds his erection slipped deeper between her legs and when this happened, she adjusted. She wanted to laugh, so mechanical was his maneuvering. Finally, she did laugh. She laughed and then laughed harder because she hadn't meant to laugh, but what were they doing anyway, she thought. How absurd the chase suddenly seemed.

"Fuck you," Max said. He stood then and paced as an embarrassed child might. "Get dressed. I'm driving you home. You're not mature enough—You're just a kid, man."

It was the *just a kid* comment that started it, that led to posting the video, and she saw that now; she'd always riled when her maturity was questioned. Even when she was nine, she'd storm throughout the house when her parents refused to let her watch an R-rated movie or go and see her favorite band at a bar when she was thirteen. Or when she was spanked for watching porn at eleven, after hours of studying video upon video of homos and heteros, cis and trans in every position. She was an old soul, her mother often told her, too confident for her age and soon, her mother said, this would get her into trouble.

Max would understand long before Ruth that her pride worked in his favor.

"Go jerk off, you dildo," she said. "We're going for pizza when you're done."

"No," he said. "No—" He couldn't finish. A blue vein tapped in time across his temple and his breathing grew hard, rapid. His entire body worked to deny an outburst, physical or verbal, Ruth could not tell. He stood this way looking to the ceiling, flexing his fingers, until he finally threw himself back onto the bed and faced the shadowed corner. "This is over," he said. "I'm too old for this shit."

Ruth had decided to sleep with him long before this final insult, but when she pulled him on top of her, his face pouty and long, she was too angry to find pleasure and instead looked forward to the moment after when she knew he would joke and talk again, and they could eat pizza and perhaps watch a movie.

The second time Ruth met with Dr. Rushani, a journalist from sororitylife.news.edu ambushed Ruth in the lobby of the nondescript corporate building and demanded an interview. She told Ruth that women suffered from revenge porn all the time and because her case was high profile, a testimony from Ruth would help hundreds of women feel less alone. She told Ruth the story was bigger than she was and that ignoring the press was irresponsible. Her mother had brought her to this meeting, the first full session, and her mother clapped this small college-aged woman away as if she were a cat sneaking bites from the leaves of a houseplant. She did not even speak when she *clap-clap-clap* backed the journalist through the wide, glass doors.

"Your mother told me about our little visitor," Dr. Rushani said. "You'll come through the service entrance from now on. You can't blame her. So many others have fallen victim to the same misogynistic stunt. Don't even get me started on the men who watch—"

"Stop."

Ruth was still very angry with Max at this time. So many people hated Max. She bathed in this knowledge, submerged her entire being into his fall.

Max wanted to do it outside, and so Ruth followed him behind the coffee shop after one of his shows and they climbed on top of a dumpster. She ignored the ribbed plastic that dug painfully into her spine. He didn't last long. He rarely did when she agreed to his many designs. By this time, she no longer protested and followed through with all of his fantasies: sex in a pool, road-head, anal, facials, and cosplay. Everything was on the table. They were exploring together, she thought, and had she any particular kink to suggest, she could have; he often begged her to consider some sexual adventure, but truthfully, she hadn't one.

Max's band had played with a new drummer, a woman with black hair, cutoffs, and a Metallica T-shirt. She wore spiked bracelets and a studded belt, and while playing, she stared down her crash cymbal with a nasty smile, as if she caused the cymbal pain and liked that she was good at hurting it. Ruth wanted to be near her, and so she helped load the drum set into Nicki's F-150. Nicki rolled a joint and smoked Ruth out in the open, sitting on the released tailgate. Max was inside talking to everyone and no one, laughing, still covered in sweat, floating from person to person, bright with praise.

"He's a cunt," Nicki said, laughing as if calling Max a cunt was the kindest thing she had said about anyone. "You're, like, still in high school, right? So, were you cherry?"

Nicki didn't expect an answer. She squinted and laughed, her laugh like a cruel sibling who wanted to gain a rise. She pinched Ruth high on the ribs. Ruth didn't laugh. She sat still and hard, trying not to blush or admit any truths to this woman: a tough woman, a drummer, a woman who held herself like a bully but teased like family.

"You smell like cum," Nicki said. "Don't worry. My sense of smell is, like, supernatural, especially when I'm lit."

Ruth leaned against Nicki's shoulder, soaked with sweat, and Nicki laid back against her kick drum guiding Ruth's head to rest on her chest. Neither said a word, strangers only moments before.

Time passed. This was how Ruth always began this part of the story in her meetings with Dr. Rushani—"time passed"— because blips on otherwise blank graphs marked the events after that night. Max was suddenly busier than he had been before, practicing, he said, until late and then drinking with the band at Lamplighter Lounge. It wasn't personal, he said. He'd make time for her that weekend. Nicki showed up at her school some after-noons, drove her to thrift stores and the record shop, and smoked her out in the bed of her truck. She laughed in that bullying way and lay to face the sky. Ruth liked spending time with Nicki, but Nicki made fun of Ruth, mocking her voice when Ruth observed two cardinals tussling for the same branch, mocking the way Ruth walked: "you look like you've just been ass-fisted"; any compliment felt like an insult: "your skin smells like downy feathers, like you've just been taken out of the box. Max is a pervert, total pedophile." But anytime Nicki called her, she went without question, laughed when Nicki teased and soon learned to keep her observations inside, to loosen her walk, to shower less so that grime obscured her complexion.

The first video she and Max made was her idea, sort of; she had hoped Max would back off from obsessing over her period. Through her entire cycle, he wanted to have sex and she let him even though it grossed her out. Afterwards, he admired his rust-colored dick and her legs and commented too many times that it was beautiful.

"I want to taste it," he said.

She refused. She dressed and spent a long time in the bathroom sitting on the toilet seat, hoping that by the time she returned, he would've moved onto something else. He hadn't. He needled.

"What's the big deal? All you have to do is lie there," he said. "You'll get an orgasm out of it; I wonder what that's like," he said, "to have an orgasm and bleed simultaneously. How's this different than anything else we've done?"

"Fine," Ruth said. "But I want to record you doing it."

Her bluff backfired. Max spent the next hour adjusting the camera and Ruth's body to get the right angle, finally deciding that it was best if she held the camera and recorded him. She had just shaved her head and the video began with him approaching her, zooming unsteadily towards her face. She took the camera away from him and filmed as he knelt between her legs.

The more he pulled away from her, the more she used the camera as a way to draw him back. The risk was higher on film, the possibilities elaborate. They often spent an entire afternoon recording as they smoked in bed, drove around, or fucked. Then Max would disappear for days. Nicki too stopped calling and often, if Ruth got Max on the phone, she could hear Nicki's laugh in the background.

When Max asked her to let Nicki join them in bed, Ruth was not surprised. He'd promised Ruth this would be the first time he and Nicki had hooked up.

"I want her, man," he told Ruth. "I don't cheat, you know. Let's, like, invite Nicki into the mix."

Ruth was amazed, smoking next to an open window and watching as Nicki and Max slept naked across from her. She was proud, she often told Dr. Rushani, that these two powerful and older people were drawn to her. For the next few weeks, Max,

Nicki, and Ruth were inseparable, and she was grateful the distance between Max and her had finally closed. This was all she cared about, her triangle. Her videos. She no longer saw friends from high school, friends she'd known since elementary. Her brother Pat wrote her letters bitching her out for ignoring him at shows, for "acting too cool," and slid them under her bedroom door until he finally stopped speaking to her altogether. She'd skipped school so often a truancy officer was called to her home. But she was happy. She loved spending days hitting up thrift stores or hanging fliers around town for shows, and she hated imagining what Max and Nicki did without her.

She often thought about the first time Max and Nicki had gone out just the two of them, reliving the furious hurt even at St. Anne's while scrubbing the floor in the morning.

"Look," Max said. "I don't want to always hang out with you *and* Nicki. Sometimes I just want to hang out with one of you alone, like, when Nicki and me go to the bar."

"We can buy booze and drink on your porch. It's cheaper."

"You're not listening. We *want* to go *without* you. It doesn't mean anything. It's just—"

"How does Nicki feel?"

"It was her idea, man. She's been bugging me for weeks, trying to get you out of the house for, like, two seconds."

Max drove Ruth home. She hadn't slept in her bed for a month. Pat ignored her and her parents didn't know she was there. She cried. She made a video with her phone of herself dancing, slowly removing one article of clothing at a time and texted it to them both. They didn't respond to the text and she couldn't sleep. At four in the morning, they showed up wasted and knocked on the basement window. After she let them in, Nicki stationed the camera on a stack of books and left it recording through the night.

The sun came up and Nicki and Max dressed while Ruth slept. Later, Ruth watched this part of the video over and over, watched how they crept around the room and told each other to shut up and giggled, and she watched as Max made a mock-sweet face and prayer hands over her sleeping body and listened as he said "what a little angel," and she listened again and again as Nicki came to her defense for a change—"You're an asshole and she could do better." Ruth watched as they each left the frame, and then she watched the next four hours of her unknowing, unmoving sleep.

"Have you heard from Max?" Dr. Rushani asked.

"No," Ruth lied.

She had received a letter from Max. He loved her, he said, and he was sorry for the way he had treated her. "Nicki is a bitch," he said. "Can I come visit? Is there anywhere private we can meet? I mean I can't stop thinking about your body, about fucking you. I haven't hooked up since going to jail. You owe me," he said, "after all I've been through. Just once, you know, for old time's sake."

She readily thought of three different places between Windell and Tacos Jalisco where they could meet—the woods outside Windell, an abandoned greenhouse behind an unused dormitory at St. Anne's, and a motel off the highway she had biked to see him. Her initial excitement was overridden, however, when she remembered the last time she saw Nicki—"Here comes little miss sunshine with her camera"—and she did not respond to Max's letter.

"Well, that's a start," Dr. Rushani said. Just like that, she said: "*A start?*" Ruth watched her face. A calm smile had replaced what Ruth now realized was tension around her lipless mouth. For a moment, it seemed Dr. Rushani didn't know how to proceed; she straightened a stack of papers on her desk, filed them in her top drawer. She sipped tea. "How are you adjusting to St. Anne's? Sister Alice says you're a model student, observant and respectful."

A start? What the fuck does "a start" mean? She stared down Dr. Rushani and with cold calculation admitted the truth. "I did it," Ruth said. In her mind's eye, she reviewed the memory as an audience might: seated at the desk in her bedroom in the dark, flipping through all the videos in a folder labeled WITH MAX until she decided on one that focused exclusively on him, showing her face briefly, before Max knelt between her legs. "I posted the video."

Pat had found the video first. Of course, he had. What fifteen-year-old wasn't scanning porn sites? He didn't show their parents, but instead he showed Tyler, a mutual friend who often drove Pat to shows once Ruth stopped hanging out with anyone besides Max and Nicki. Tyler sent the link to Ruth's mother. But her parents were afraid the cops would charge them because they'd let the relationship go on for so long, and it was ultimately her brother who imitated a concerned father and told the police where to find the two together. Nicki was not with them when the cops showed up at Max's house. She was not in the video Ruth had posted, and so no one knew to involve Nicki. The trial was an uneventful statutory rape case where Ruth's opinion didn't matter and Max's prosecution was in the hands of people who knew nothing of their relationship. Then Tyler wrote an essay about revenge porn for *Art in Action* that was subsequently picked up by *Slate* and *Buzzfeed* and then everywhere else in the country, even sororitylife.news.edu. Tyler hadn't known the details and so she embellished: *My close friend since grade school fell prey to an older, respected punk in the scene who refused to let her see her friends, who shaved her head even though she didn't want him to, who manipulated her into various sex acts, and who eventually convinced her to film their private lives all under the guise of it being just for him.* Media came through town like a firestorm. Max was sentenced to a year in county and was designated as a sex offender. Ruth's parents enrolled her in Catholic School.

"That isn't funny, Ruth," Dr. Rushani said. "I don't like being mocked. If you can't take this seriously, I'll have to recommend a different psychiatrist. That means I will hand over my notes to someone else, perhaps even your mother, depending on how she wants to proceed."

Ruth did not argue her case in this immaculate and dim room.

"Oh, Ruth. When will you stop defending him?"

Max *had* been the one to share the videos first, just not so publicly. One afternoon, during the period when he was ignoring her and she could not get him to commit to a date, she showed up at his house unannounced. His bicycle was on the porch, Nicki's truck was in the driveway, and when she let herself in through the front door and climbed the stairs to his room, she smelled weed and heard laughter. She opened the door, expecting to see Nicki and Max where they often sat at a small table next to the open windows, but instead Scotty was there, and the three were lying on Max's bed watching a video of Ruth giving Max a blowjob. She remembered this moment well. Scotty jumped from the bed and apologized, twice, as he left the room. Nicki laughed; Max looked angry.

And now she raged internally; she felt so fucking alone. There was no one but Max, the one person she should not see, who should not want to see her. They were tied, exiled as victim and perpetrator, and jailed by the truth that these titles fluctuated. He had not told on her, after all; what good would it have done? Yet, she still hated him, her body no longer her own. They had been building what she thought of as a pile of gifts to consider in time and each rearrangement was made worth it by this togetherness. She knew now he had not seen it in this way, had not seen her as permanent. Why else would he turn to Nicki? She understood her presence as fleeting when recalling his words: *you're just a kid. We want,* he said, *without you.* She had destroyed his life, she knew, but he had done the same to her.

She left Dr. Rushani's office and walked down the service stairs. When she arrived at St. Anne's, Ruth asked Sister Alice if she could use the public phone to call her mother even though it was evening.

"Speak softly, and don't stay on too long," Sister Alice said.

Ruth dialed Max's house first but got no answer; receiver in hand, finger on the cool metal tongue. She dialed Tacos Jalisco.

Max agreed to meet her the following Saturday at the motel off the highway she rode north of Windell.

She counted the yellow dashes, concentrating now, keeping four and then five in her mind so that she would not forget. This way she remained blank, singing nothing but the numbers, her breathing like a metronome. At first, when the dividing lines connected into parallels, she exhaled powerfully, as if the count was physically taxing. By the second mile, however, minutes away from the motel where Max waited, the count matched the rhythm of her bicycle chain clicking around the rear hub, and she moved from one through ten without forgetting where she had started or where she meant to end. And it was then, in this meditative space, that she heard what sounded like screaming: vocals torn and peaked, human but not. She listened, searched the pine grove that ran the length of the highway.

Ahead of her, in the lane for oncoming traffic, was a crow.

A car crested uphill, a dot at first, and colorless but for the sun glare. Ruth threw down her bike and ran, but the sedan, now full blue with chrome and a single driver, split the distance and they passed one another at the exact place where the crow struggled. The scream that erupted from the bird after the car had driven over the wing was the sound of pain: universal and nonverbal. Ruth saw something shoot from beneath the wheel. The crow struggled, free now. All around was a deep red, but too bright and synthetic to be blood. The same color covered the crow's torso; it was paint. Her breath smoked, and another car bore down on them, and she ripped off her sweater and wrapped the crow tightly, staunching the blood. When the car passed, she saw that one of the bird's wings was stripped to the bone and covered in latex paint. A few feet away, a silver lid reflected the sun.

Ruth did not know if crows cried, but there were tears in the black eyes and the beak worked silently through pain; she did not know how to tell the gender of the black bird either, but the word Edie appeared in her mind and that seemed like a fine designation.

"Hello Edie," and she spread the damaged wing and saw where three hooked bones had snapped. On the side of the highway, Ruth tore the cover from a hardback she'd been reading and pressed the binder's board against the flattened, wounded wing, wrapping it tightly with her scarf. For a moment, she thought of walking Edie to the motel where Max waited. He did have more freedom than her, after all, but she recoiled at an image of him reaching out and touching Edie, of him cooing and comforting the crow.

Ruth smuggled Edie into St. Anne's, hidden beneath her sweaters against her breast, and when the two were caught later that night, she quit school, taking her GED the following spring. Throughout her slow but steady climb from community college to a BA, and eventually, an MFA in film from NYU—even after her first documentary about interspecies communication screened at Sundance—Ruth never forgot the fragility of Edie's broken wing, a touch-memory that lingered as the coarse handfuls of Max's hair had once.

SHADOW PLAY

SHADOW PLAY

BEFORE BOBBY VANISHED, him and me sold plastics to the Shade Point PD in exchange for candy corn, chocolate bars, and chewing gum. Our go-to guy, Lieutenant Hurns, was a two-ton boa constrictor with jack-o'-lantern eyes, but he always took our goods. I'd known "The Boa" since my days on the force, back before I got canned. Back before I became a private eye and took up the junk trade. We scavenged, mostly—Bobby and me. Dumpsters, vacant houses, and the occasional big lift from department stores kept us in steady supply. Usually we got The Boa strong fibered stuff like Honey Walkers, Catalina Black Cats, and Potato Heads. I prided myself on doing good business. Treat a customer right and he'll come back—that's what Sarge always said.

Two days had passed since me and Bobby fought over priorities. Bobby wanted to diversify, and I wanted to stay the boss.

"We gotta beef up our angle," he'd said. "Every urchin out there is diving for plastics."

"Beef up, say?" What could Bobby, who weighed eighty-two pounds, possibly know about beefing?

"Norm, it's all we can do to stay afloat—"

"That's it? You're scared of The Boa," I said. "We keep his belly full, so nothing stirs."

"Yeah, well. What if I want to be boss for a change?" He kicked my desk, scuffed the white rubber of his Converse.

I turned my swivel chair to face the wall and said, "Let me alone, Bobby." He made for the door. "Not there." I pointed to the fire escape. "There," I said, and made him leave through the window to show him I was still boss.

Normally we hawked junk-goods on the street where no one cared what they got, just so long as they got it. But later that night, Bobby took a junk supply of pick-up sticks to The Boa, and that was the last time I laid eyes on him.

I needed to get this thing ironed out, and so I picked up the Campbell's direct that ran across the alley to The Boa's lair. I rang the loose bells on his end. After the third jingle, he picked up.

"What do you want, Norman?" I hated his voice, shrill like a crow-call.

"Where's Bobby?" I asked. Direct. That's what The Boa responded to.

"Norman. Stop this, okay? Like, you know where Bobby is."

"All I know is I sent Bobby to you and now he's—"

The Boa coughed, and his voice turned wet. "Mom!" he yelled and dropped the line.

After that I decided to call the one person I could trust— Sarge. I rang bells on our special line, the Green Giant direct, and he picked up on the first jingle.

He said, "Norm, your mother wants you to come down and eat dinner."

"No time to eat, Sarge. I'm in a bind," I said. "Bobby's missing. I called The Boa, but turned up loose leaves." I waited to see what Sarge would say, if he knew anything or not. "I need your advice."

The Sarge inhaled. He always inhaled when he needed me to understand something fully. "Norm." He paused. There was some rustling, and the Green Giant cable moved up and down on my end. I imagined him lifting his glasses and rubbing the red pockmarks on his nose. He said, "When we don't quite understand something, we have to backtrack. Retrace our steps."

"Backtrack, say?"

"Norman," he said. "When you find Bobby, are you prepared for what that might mean?"

"He's my partner," I said.

"Come down to dinner, son."

Was he crazy? Who could eat at a time like this? *Bobby's out there, and someone's gotta know where.* I'd have to go to The Boa myself. I needed to think. *Retrace my steps.* The last time I saw Bobby was after our fight. He waved goodbye from the fire escape stairs. He wore a blue-and-red knit hat and his fur-lined bomber jacket. Something was off, though. He didn't have on his shark-tooth necklace, but I saw him wearing it earlier that day when we played ball out front of Headquarters. Bobby only took off his lucky shark tooth when he got mad at God. He often threw heat against God, but he always told me why. Like he couldn't play professional baseball on account of his mismatched legs. One foot stopped three inches shy of the other. He also got low on air sometimes. Once, his sister, Betty, dressed him up like some two-bit Raggedy Ann and forced him to drink tea. Halfway through an imaginary crumpet his lungs gave out, and an ambulance drove him to the hospital while he was wearing a dress and bonnet. Saddest day of my life, seeing my partner hauled away all dolled up like that.

At my desk, I turned on the world lamp and pulled out a Buck Rogers scratch pad. I wrote "Missing Shark Tooth." Things were getting deep. I had nothing to go on and needed more clues. I wrote down "The Boa." Shaking a cup full of throwing dice, I closed my eyes—*If not The Boa, then who?*

A knock brought me back. *One. Two. Three. One. Two.*

"Come in," I shouted.

A woman walked in with a dropped smile and fat lips, looking like every person who ever came through my door. What this time? Lost dog? Sister out with Benny Price? Any number of woes could hang on the back of a dame in this city. She looked familiar, like I knew her from somewhere back in time—yellow summer dress, a blue apron with white paisley flowers, a mop of blonde curls around her forehead. Gray eyes.

"Norman?" she said.

"That's me," I said.

"You have to help me understand, honey," she said. "I need your help."

Every person who walked through that door needed my help, and I told each one, "It'll cost you."

"Norman!"

"Detective Norman," I corrected her.

"I see," she said. "It's about Bobby—"

"My partner?" I said. "What is this?"

"He's gone, honey."

"I know he's gone. I've been racking my pool balls trying to retrace my steps. Where is he? Does The Boa have him?"

"Betty hates it when you call her that, Norman. You know she does," the woman said.

"Betty-shmetty. Where's Bobby!?"

There was a quick knock at the door, and Sarge walked in. Always in the nick. I had a feeling he'd dig up some dirt.

"He's a detective," the woman said in a grumpy tone I didn't much care for.

Sarge nodded. He would know how to get answers out of her. "Detective Norman, I have a case for you," he said. "It won't be easy."

The woman blew air from her nose like a horse before the cavalry charge.

"I accept your job with utmost care," I said. "But as you can see, I have one distressed dame to look after first." *Treat a customer right, and he'll come back.*

"Norman! Don't refer to me as *dame*," the woman said.

"Detective," Sarge said, "I know this woman, and that's part of your assignment."

"Bobby?" I mumbled.

Sarge nodded.

The dame turned cat eyes on Sarge and said, "James, stop!" *She knew something, but what did she know?*

Sarge continued, "As always, you're the only one who can handle the job."

The woman walked toward the door. "James," she said. "In the hall."

Sarge held a finger up to his nose, secret code for play it cool. I did the same.

The two went into the hall and shut the door. I turned off the lamp so I could snoop. They whispered, but I made an ear horn with my Buck Rogers scratch pad and caught some clues: *Two Bones and The Miller.*

They stopped whispering. I turned the world lamp back on and waited.

"We're ironed out," Sarge said. "Let's get down to business."

The woman ran her fingers through her hair and rubbed the corners of her eyes. When she brought her hands away tears had wet her cheeks. "No one is getting down to any business until we eat and get some sleep," she said. "That's final."

Sarge nodded in agreement. He squeezed her shoulder, but she jerked away from him leaving the door open on her way out.

I wanted to ask Sarge what kind of turkey business this "Two Bones and The Miller" meant, but something cold in his eyes kept me from trusting him in that moment. The way he'd acted with the dame, something was fish-eyed, and I couldn't risk it. Bobby's life depended on me.

"That woman knows something," I said.

Sarge looked flushed, seasick—like when he and Bobby and I were out on the ferry and the Sarge barfed after a guy, asleep on the deck, crapped his pants. The man didn't wake up or even notice. Sarge hugged iron, heaving over the deck's edge while

Bobby, quick on his feet, tossed a soda in the soiled man's face. The guy jumped at Bobby. "Who are you to stop time!" the man yelled. And just like that, time stopped.

In my office, Sarge said, "Bobby isn't with us anymore."

"I had a feeling. That Time Jumper from the ferry?"

Sarge smiled, but he wasn't happy.

Before dawn the next morning, I crawled out onto the fire escape and looked back through the window into the office me and Bobby shared for all those years. The lights were off, and I thought of Bobby standing where I stood, waving goodbye. It was dark inside and out. I traveled light, a leather satchel packed with a flashlight, rubber pencil, Buck Rogers scratch pad, high-quality plastics, my lucky silver dollar, and a handful of Atomic Fireballs.

I needed to see The Boa.

To reach his lair, I had to climb down to street level, crawl through a break in the chain-link fence, and walk up two flights on the fire escape. The other option, walking all the way around to the front, was out of the question. Back in first grade, a Jumper trapped me in shadow, and by the time I busted loose he'd managed to steal my jacket and shoes. It was Bobby's idea to never go solo on that dark path, and I hadn't set foot up the fence line ever since, except once, the same day of our fight, when Bobby fell during our ball game. Running after a fly ball, he tripped on his tall shoe and hit the ground so hard you could hear his hip smack asphalt for miles around. He slung his arm over my neck, and I shouldered him back up the fire escape to our Headquarters.

Once I reached The Boa's entrance, I tapped the secret knock with my finger and waited. *One. One. One.* Nothing. *One. One. One.* Nothing. *One*—the window flung open, and The Boa stuck his head out—long blonde hair, triangular eyes.

"Norm!" The Boa said. "Like, stop. Okay. Leave me out of this." He paused, looked me over. "Whatever *this* is."

"You know where Bobby is. Now spill!"

"Stop, okay. Just cut it out," The Boa said. "You and your stupid games."

"This is serious. What do you know about The Miller? Or Two Bones?" I took the rubber pencil from my leather satchel. The Boa closed the window and walked out of his room.

"Not so easy," I said. I tapped, waited, and then tapped again—*One. One. One.*—but The Boa didn't return.

Out on the street, shadows hovered around lampposts: Time Jumpers. I could feel them. Nasty like split-pea soup, dirty like the man who pooped himself on the ferry. To be safe, I kept in the light and away from walls and bushes. Bobby had a keen ear for Jumpers; at any moment he'd turn to me and say, "Let's go, Norman. I don't like it here." I'd listen because although Bobby was a year younger than me, he had intuition. Christmas, a few years back, he knew exactly what Santa had brought me. When I asked him how, he just shrugged and said, "I guessed." But I knew he had rare gifts other people often overlooked on account of his short leg. I hoped the Jumpers hadn't found out, too.

Garbage collectors were out on the street. I pulled my hood down over my eyes—garbage men and me were on the sharp edge of a fence since I broke into their racket without paying dues. In the window of the wig shop that ran under The Boa's place, a gray manne-quin face sported a foot-tall bouffant; another had an ear-length bob like Bobby's ma, Mrs. Tulane. They looked more robot than human.

Once the garbage men passed, I kicked at a pile of damp leaves mounded against the curb. Damp leaves held secrets. One day the crows were digging around—"What are they doing that for?" I'd asked Sarge. "They saw something shiny," he said. From then on Bobby and me left no pile unturned, and we came out spoiled most of the time. I peeped around for shadows overhead. Jumpers could nab you anywhere, and *Bang!* I saw a restaurant sign—TWO BONES BBQ. If I had the right Two Bones, then Bobby didn't make it very far. The Jumpers must have had set-eyes on Headquarters, already had set-eyes on Bobby.

Two Bones BBQ sat at the intersection of Madison and Doyle. A stoplight changed from yellow to red, and a black Chrysler drove fast down Madison and nearly lost control when it turned too tight on Doyle just in front of me. I jumped away from the road and crouched against the building. I heard a scream like a hurt dog—high and cut short—but it was just the car as it fishtailed out of there. When I looked up, there was nothing but dark road.

As I shook the screaming tires from my mind, I brushed off the grime that muddied my knees and rear. I was glad Bobby hadn't seen me turn chicken. He needed me to be tough, especially now.

Two Bones was shut up tight. There were no store hours posted, just a dark dining room with round booth seats and big tables. The place stunk of Time Jumpers. Cobwebs hung around the entranceway, and empty bottles were strewn at my feet.

I left the front and ran through the dark alley that separated Two Bones from the neighboring housing complex. Around back, I found a metal dumpster full of rotting smells and cardboard boxes. But before I could investigate further, I heard the crackle of feet on dried leaves. An old man stood, rubbing his hands against the cold.

"Been shut down about four years now," he said. Loose skin hung from his neck, and his teeth moved with his lips as he talked.

"Years, say?" The shadows stretched over us.

"I remember taking my son here, when his mama had to work. Lou would set him up with a bowl of banana pudding." The old man stared up toward Doyle. "Damn shame," he said. "Bobby, I mean."

Dirty rotten Jumper, always gaining a rise.

"What'd'ya do with Bobby!?"

"Norm, that's not fair," he said. "You know very well what happened to Bobby."

"Do I? Listen, Jumper, I'm tight with The Boa."

Looking toward the corner of Madison and Doyle, the old man seemed lost in thought. I followed his gaze down the alley. Shadows had broken in places.

"Your father's damned half-baked scheme," the old man said. "Won't tell you the truth. Don't want anybody else to say nothing. I say bullshit!" He spat on the ground. "You won't find Bobby in this world," he told me. "That's for certain."

"Tell me what world he's in then! You've had your fun."

"You want to know, Norm? Go down to the Millers. Ask them—"

"Millers!" I said. "Where's The Miller?"

The old Jumper told me I could find The Miller at the corner of Peabody and Third. It took the better part of an hour to hike downtown. The Miller's stone building had no windows, and if it weren't for a little wooden sign hung over the door, I would've barreled right past the place.

The doorknob below the Millers' sign wiggled but didn't give me any inches. I rubbed between the stones. Sarge always said to study cracks. The stones stopped and became an alley.

A tiny door was hinged inside of a larger garage gate that took up most of the alley wall. I tried my luck and found the small door unlocked. Inside were two long station wagons with no windows except for in the front. A platform elevator, held together by chains and pulleys, sat next to a stack of slender, long wooden crates.

I was getting a plug on The Miller.

The elevator raised me into a blinding, bright room. When my vision cleared, I made out plastic containers of liquid pumping through large metal machines. I was so distracted at first that I didn't notice that each fluid connected to tubes, and those tubes fed into a person. Someone had stuffed a fat man inside of a clear plastic sleeping bag and laid him out on his back. A smell like gasoline hung around his body. I poked the man's belly, but his fat made no waves. The man was stiff as rubber. *Zombie slaves?*

I felt a biting deep in my lungs and feared for Bobby.

An office sat across from the zombie ward. I took note of a desk and books but didn't pilfer. I kept my back flat to the corridor wall and soft-shoed up to a door with a large window. Inside, oven doors lined white walls. I held my breath deep down the way Sarge taught me and mental-named the Mets' players until I felt brave again.

The first thing I noticed inside the room was the cold. I had chill-bumps and could see the smoke from my lungs. On a few of the oven doors there hung clipboards and papers. One clipboard read Donna Earley and had numbers and letters written in pencil. *Jumper code.* Afraid that zombies were just behind those little doors, I wanted to scram, but a clipboard next to Zombie Donna raised my hat—Bobby-Jean Tulane.

I thought of the fat man all plugged up to those machines and taking zombie juice through high-quality plastics. *Is Bobby next in line, or am I too late?* My heart hummed like the ferry engine as it pushed through the bay. My ears rushed with a noise like water breaking open against the stern. *Them dirty Jumpers will pay if Bobby ain't Bobby-proper no more.* I jerked at the door handle, but it was jammed. I planted my feet on the wall and yanked. Nothing. My leverage was all wrong. But I ain't the boss for growing moss, and so I had the good sense to nab a chair from that office I peeped down the hall.

Once I got the chair situated under the drawer, I took hold of the handle. After a few more pulls the drawer eased out with a loud squeal, and cold smoke billowed around the opening. An atomic burn swelled up from my throat, and I nearly lost the stash of fireballs I'd munched along the way when I saw Bobby zipped up in a clear plastic sleeping bag. Sarge gave me tricks to stop the drummer boy from beating his way out of my chest—counting, breathing, naming ball players—but Bobby's face looked distorted through the milky plastic, gray like the mannequin heads at the wig shop.

"No tin-heart Jumper's turning my partner into a zombie slave!" I yelled, and my voice echoed in the white room long after I unzipped the part covering Bobby's head. Slowly I put my hand to his mouth and felt for breath, but his face was so cold I withdrew.

Not in this world. That's what the old Jumper had said. It all clicked, then. Bobby's body was in a frozen state, in this world, in this time, but where was his mind? I knew I had to wake him up to bring him back, *but how?*

When we scavenged, back before Bobby disappeared, I could lift him up on my back if his leg gave out. The day he tripped we were playing ball, Bobby refused to let me carry him home— "Let me alone," he said. "I ain't no wimp." He gripped my hand, and I shouldered him to the sidewalk before nabbing the baseball from where it rolled on the other side of Doyle. He wasn't no wimp, and I never said he was. I just got used to carrying him is all. But as I gripped the plastic seam around his shoulders and pulled, I couldn't drag him loose. He was triple weight.

"Come on, Bobby," I said. My elbows ached in the cold as if I had a fever. "You want to be boss, you got to help me out on this." I felt too much drumming, like I might pass out from too much air, but I didn't give up. Instead, I climbed on the shelf where he lay to gain better leverage.

I'd never paid much attention to Bobby's short leg. Unless you looked at his tall shoe, the one with rubber heels three inches high, you'd never know the difference. But somehow it seemed wrong to touch his short leg, naked under the plastic, and so I pushed at the other. The lower half of his body slid out and away from the shelf where he lay, but didn't drop. Instead, as if an invisible board held him aloft, he levitated. I jumped back down on the chair. Grabbing Bobby's feet, I yanked at him in jerky little movements, sliding his body off the shelf one inch at a time.

I'd nearly freed Bobby when The Miller stalked through the door wearing a white coat over a brown suit and tie. "What's the idea, kid?" The Miller stared at me and then Bobby. "Get away from that body!"

I held out the office chair like a lion tamer. "Don't try and stop me," I said, sounding confident but shaking all over. "I've come for Bobby."

The Miller sidestepped my thrashing chair but took a hit in his hip. This made him bigger, and he pushed the chair into my chest. I staggered back and watched as he put Bobby's feet back onto the shelf and zipped the plastic bag. I couldn't stop him. I couldn't. He stood ten feet above any man. I watched him shut Bobby back up into the wall. A loud *boom* echoed throughout the chamber.

"Listen, kid," he said and pointed into the room. "You can't be in here."

The Miller had a stuttering problem. Every time he began to talk, he paused. My guess, too many years bouncing time. I had a stuttering problem once, but Dr. Horowitz cured it by making me read Sherlock Holmes out loud with marbles stuffed in my mouth.

With the chair held out against The Miller, I moved closer to Bobby's drawer. Me and The Miller locked eyes. For a Jumper he had nice eyes—like my mother's. I couldn't look away. *Hypnotism.* Bobby's way of blocking hypnotism was to close his eyes and scream.

"ABCDEFGHIJKLMNOP—" I yelled with my peepers locked tight.

"Kid. Kid!" The Miller said, shaking me. He cut the slow-stutters. Messing up his hypnotism really got him riled. I pushed the chair into his stomach and cocked back once more, landing a direct hit across his arm.

"Goddamn," The Miller said.

I hightailed it out of there—back through the Zombie Ward, down the elevator, and through the little door.

Out on Peabody, I tore rubber and reached Third Street in no time flat. Halfway home, there was an army of filthy Jumpers in the dark parking lot of Joe's Liquor, and I knelt in the shadow waiting for them to take me, but each Jumper shuffled under the yellow and green of Joe's neon sign and made no moves. "Trade me out," I yelled at the Jumpers, and a lady Jumper said, "Get on home. Ain't no place for games and such." The whole trek home I stayed in the shadows, but nothing happened. No Jumper came.

No shadows opened. Bobby had been so close and *poof* I lost him. We fought over plastics. I made him leave down the fire escape to show him who was boss. Then, he got nabbed. Disappeared. Not in this world.

At the corner of Madison and Doyle, in front of Two Bones BBQ, I saw Bobby standing there as if waiting on me. He wore the same bomber jacket and white shoes. My ears boomed with ocean sounds, waves on waves breaking against rock to make sand, and my voice sounded hollow, like screaming underwater, as I called, "Bobby! I've been combing for you."

He said nothing, and so I said, "You got nothing to say?"

But he ran, and I bolted after him. We passed my cousin Lucy's house. Then we passed Bobby's music teacher's house. "Bobby, goddamn it!" I yelled, like The Miller had. "Stop running!" The kid slowed at Headquarters, below Bobby's apartment and in front of the wig shop and Two Bones BBQ, and I saw then that it wasn't Bobby at all, but a neighborhood boy named Ralph. "Fuck off, Norman!" Ralph said.

I bent over. With my hands spread across my knees, I felt icicles scrape up through my throat.

Ralph ran home, and I didn't chase after him.

I yelled and threw myself down on the street once I was outside of Bobby's apartment. The shadows were dark and heavy over me. "Goddamn it, Bobby—" I struck the asphalt. "Open up, you shit-stained Jumpers!" I punched and punched until I saw blood on my knuckles. And then, like a smack to the head, I remembered seeing Bobby's shark tooth on the road after he'd tripped. *Daft!* His shark tooth was what he went after, that night, in the road. Must've come unhitched when Bobby dove for the fly ball. Before our fight, before The Miller.

People crowded around me, looking on as I combed the scene for Bobby's lucky shark tooth among the flecks of gold and silver mixed in the asphalt, but I couldn't make out faces. A man grabbed my shoulders and tried to pull me off the ground. I swung my arms around and beat him back—"Gotta find it," I said. And below the TWO BONES BBQ sign sat the pile of leaves I had noticed that morning. They looked so dark, wet, but something shined on the inside and I saw it shine. Crawling past the people, around their leather shoes and house slippers, I reached the sidewalk and dug through the leaves. They mushed like putty as I curled my fingers around a silver chain and pulled up Bobby's shark tooth.

"Norman," Sarge said and laid his weight into me. He smelled like Old Spice and felt like a heavy blanket. "Come on," he said. "Let's go inside."

"Bobby's—" I choked and didn't say more.

Bobby's sister, Betty, said, "Like probably not the best idea to be in the road, especially after Bobby got hit, you know."

Sarge lifted me off the ground. I hugged his neck and buried my face into his shirt. My breathing drew short like Bobby's would when he lost air. My mother wrapped her arms around Sarge and me. Her dress smelled like pot roast. "He's gone," I said. "Bobby's gone," I said again just to hear the words come out of my mouth. The three of them, my mother, Sarge, and Betty, walked me toward home, toward Headquarters. I watched all of our feet moving together. Between their bodies, I could see the street, and even though we stood in shadow, the Jumpers dared not move.

HALLELUJAH **STATION**

HALLELUJAH STATION

BEFORE MY HUSBAND, Manny Sylvester, rescued me and caused my second electrocution, he did not believe in miracles. Nor did I. But it *is* a miracle that I am baking a cake for our anniversary while Manny listens to an LP recording of Bing Crosby's "Did You Ever See a Dream Walking?" I love Crosby—*dAdo–dadAdoo*—and Manny knows it, too. The first time he entered my little attic room at Holy Oaks Asylum, Manny whistled the same song, a song I heard nightly on one of the various radio transmissions I received through my teeth.

I hadn't felt the touch of another in years, not since my mother had lathered my hair with shampoo, her hands like catcher's mitts pawing my child-scalp. I jerked away from her, and the pink radio fell into my bathwater. Next time I opened my eyes and saw the world, I was in a hospital, and I had breasts and underarm hair: a vegetable. Not my term—the hospital staff called me "Cucumber" on account of my feet turning green if no one massaged blood down into them.

For a time, I had a roommate named Martha. Each night the nurses wrapped me tightly in blankets, but one night Martha stole my afghan, and I fell headfirst onto the linoleum floor. That's

when The Girl appeared. Suddenly, she was there, a girl just like
me but slouched in the corner of a room I imagined in my mind.
It has always been hard to explain The Girl. You see, she *was* me,
of course, but at the time I saw her as someone independent of me.
Before her, I was barely aware of my surroundings and her arrival
ushered in my return, or rather, mirrored it. Her room began as
just a dark cave with none of the pretty bedding or furniture she
later trucked in from someplace. She shivered under all that lank,
dirty hair covering her face. I grew more anxious after the fall,
scared of The Girl. I threw up many times a day. Martha would
paint my face with the bile before any nurses came, and so they
moved me to the attic.

The Girl and I found the radio transmission months later,
I recall, after Nurse Bruchard had finished with my bath. She was
a heavyset woman with the biggest breasts I'd ever seen, and The
Girl had stuffed pillows in her nightgown and as she acted out
Nurse Bruchard's clumsy body, my mouth fell open as if I too might
laugh: and *radio*—just like that. From then on, The Girl was downright sassy. No more cowering and brooding in the corner.

The day Manny appeared, Nurse Bruchard had abandoned
me, as was her way, next to the attic window until lunchtime. I had
not yet learned to steer the radio stations, and so circumstances
obliged me to listen to any available frequency. On that particular
afternoon, I was enjoying a Kentucky weather report about a
ravenous tornado while The Girl, the bratty pacer, clogged her
ears and sulked. She hated talk radio almost as much as she
balked at that tiny room of hers: royal blue throw rug, brass bed,
and transistor radio on the vanity where she spent most of her
days primping. Yet we both loved those late nights, long after
Nurse Bruchard had put us to bed, when my teeth played old love
songs. The Girl would dance and twirl herself around like a first-
rate prom queen.

But when Manny sauntered into the attic, the DJ was
describing a dismembered Wonder Bread truck, ripped in two,

the front end three miles from the cargo hold without a driver in sight—*as if the deliveryman had simply vanished into the dust.* Manny whistled—*dAdo-dadAdoo*—in time with sounds of mop water slopping across the tiled floor.

I shut down the transmission.

The Girl rocked on the bed; her face so close to her folded-up knees, I could not see her eyes beneath blonde bangs.

The floorboards creaked behind me, but as I was facing the window, I could not see Manny approach. He took a few careful steps closer.

"D'ya say something?" he asked.

When I didn't respond, Manny rested his mop against the wall and squatted down in front of me. His irises were black with thick gray sacks under his eyes. The way he looked at me expressed both curiosity and longing. Everyone else who visited—doctors, nurses, and orderlies—paid attention to the necessary parts of my body required for their task, but no one *looked* at me. Manny sought out my blue eyes from where my head slouched down toward my chest, a sling of drool bridging between my cheek and shoulder. Then he laughed, looked out the window.

"I'm hearing things."

A bus arrived out front, long and yellow and full of other invalids like me, who, unlike me, were taken on field trips to the zoo or Burger King. The Girl doubled over with laughter when Martha, my old roommate, punched Nurse Price in the butt. I saw the humor, but The Girl's laugh had more malice than I thought prudent. Besides, if it weren't for Martha, The Girl and I might not have discovered one another, or the radio signals, for that matter.

"Nearly forgot where I was," Manny said, staring out the window.

When he stood up, his hand accidentally brushed my knee, and I swear! I felt a current run through my skin, and The Girl went plumb crazy. She jumped and kicked and threw herself onto the bed with such force, I thought the frame might buckle.

But the look on Manny's face showed something like disgust as he wiped his hand again and again on the thigh of his jeans. I had no way of knowing this then, of course, but poor Manny despises physical contact. It isn't germs or anything like that, no, he squirms the way someone might at the idea of eating snails or squid while others revel at the delicacy. He gained his composure and sought my eyes once more and it was like we shared something beyond touch or movement.

"Poor girl," Manny said and stood up. "What you do so wrong as to be shoved up here?"

Manny drew phlegm up from his throat, a distasteful honking, and turned to leave. I was still in awe of the sensation I'd felt from his touch, accidental or otherwise, for I'd definitely felt some pulse where he'd touched. The Girl felt it too. Her hair a mess as she grabbed up the little transistor and flipped it on.

—::: *Storms of this magnitude happen frequently down in the plains, but up in the Blue Ridge, Sam. Hardly ever* :::—

Manny squatted down, again.

"That you?" he asked. "You got a radio in there?"

—::: *Old gymnasium torn right through the middle. Strangest sight. Both basketball goals still standing while all else faces God* :::—

"S'you!" he said. "Hell. What else you got on there?"

—::: *bridge collapsed. Sixteen known fatalities. The town is in shock* :::—

Sitting at her vanity, The Girl spun the radio dial forward and back, searching for a new station, and she continued to do so long after the sound of Manny's steps faded from the room.

The next time Manny visited, I'd just received a sponge bath. Nurse Bruchard had dressed me in a nightgown and laid me out flat on my back until supper. The radio played "Sleepwalk"—a melodious tune that caused The Girl to stare off into some lonely distance. But when Manny walked in, she bounced out of the chair and began fixing her hair and smoothing her dress.

Manny leaned over my bed. Although his teeth were yellowed and chipped, his smile beamed when he said, "You got oldies!"

The Girl turned her nose up as if to say, "See. No one else likes the weather."

He sat next to my bed on a small wooden chair. My head lay in such a way that I couldn't see him. Hoping he'd stand back up, I clenched my jaw and turned off the radio—a trick The Girl and I had figured out the night of our first transmission. With the radio off, Manny grew anxious. He hovered over my bed as if by simply staring he could determine if I had a loose wire. He knelt at the foot of the bed. I saw him perfectly, a man groomed by sadness. "Want me to leave? That it?" he asked.

I clenched my jaw and turned the radio back on.

"You got to be lonely up here, little lady. Where'd your family get off to?"

Where they got off to, I don't know, and at some point, I stopped caring. Maybe I even understood. My body didn't move. They had no idea my mind worked. That I said *I love you; I'm here, Mama,* over and over every time they visited. How could they've known? Only if The Girl had appeared before they had given up. The rowdier she grew, the more I felt small flashes of physical sensation shoot through me. Not that I'd want to relive that nasty fall in the old dorm after Martha had stolen my afghan.

"Did You Ever See a Dream Walking?" came on the radio. Manny clapped his hands together and yelled *whoop!* "This was my memaw's favorite song."

—::: *Did you ever see a dream talking? Well, I did* :::—

He slow danced with an invisible partner, and I wished I could've filled that space between his arms and chest. The Girl danced as if her body leaned against his, and I thought about when she first showed up, how hard things had been.

Bing Crosby rolled over into Sinatra, who became Jackie Wilson, and I watched Manny twirl and dip, careful not to hit his head on the low-pitched ceiling. The Girl struggled to hold his pace, to learn his steps. We were all so caught up in the music that the nurse, who had come to feed me, nearly found us together. I cut the music just in time, and Manny tiptoed to the closet.

I hated mealtime. The nurse tilted my head back, opened my mouth, shoved a spoonful of food in, and rotated my jaw. After a few chews, she rubbed at my throat until I swallowed. This went on until I'd eaten the green, yellow, and white mush. Then she wheeled me to the attic window, where I typically sat until bedtime.

Once she left, Manny crept from the closet. I picked up talk radio. A sermon.

—::: *The end is nigh, brothers and sisters. Forsake the body. Rapture approaches!* :::—

Not two days later, Manny announced he'd been fired.

"Little Friar Tuck thinks he can boss every damn thing," he said, pacing up to the little window and back down to my bed, where I lay after my evening bath. Charlie Parker's "Summertime" began right as Manny entered the room, but he was too angry to notice.

"Told him, I did. Said, 'You think I don't know how long my lunch s'posed to be?'" Manny yelled. "I said, 'I'm the one s'posed to eat the damn thing under thirty!'"

When he looked toward my face, I saw guilt replace the angry lines around his mouth. "Can't stand the thought of you being locked up in this tower. Damn shame us meeting like this, me down on my luck and you, well, downer on yours." He paced; a conspiratorial look in his eyes. "Want to get out of here?"

When we arrived at his large farmhouse, I felt dizzy by the romance of it all. Manny had hidden in the closet and waited for night, and just like that, he wheeled me out the service entrance. No witnesses. He was strong then, and lifted my chair into the bed of his truck with little effort, strapped me down with a length of chain. I'd nearly bumped all the way from my chair by the time we traversed those backcountry roads I now know so well. The Girl sat on her bed with a plaid suitcase at her feet, wearing a yellow summer dress that showed too much cleavage for my taste.

Once home, Manny carried me inside, wheelchair and all, and placed me next to a recliner. He sat down and leaned forward in anticipation. I also waited, but for different reasons, as my body had nearly slid to the floor. The Girl covered her face, embarrassed by my fallen posture. Manny did not want to take hold of my body. He vacillated, his fingers flitting like moths around a lamp. Eventually, he pulled a throw from the back of the couch and, covering my shoulders, pulled me upright and straightened my head as best anybody could. With that, I tuned in, but only received static. Manny turned my chair so it faced the wall, then the front door: static.

The Girl flipped through the radio dial—*chchch*—again—*chchch*.

Manny bustled around the house—so many doors opening and closing. He went upstairs and stomped through each room. I waited for him to come back and The Girl crossed her arms; her lips set to pout.

"All the genius!" Manny yelled. "Got it."

What he "got," he did not say. He lifted me from my chair in such haste that he didn't notice that my chin rested in the crook of his neck. Manny carried me up to the attic where there was an unattached wood-burning stove and an unplumbed bathtub where he placed me. My body was as light and unstructured as a blanket, and so I slid into the curved porcelain.

"Here," he said, and pulled me upright, and only then did he react. He wiped his hand on his jeans.

I tuned in. No sound save static. From where I lay, I could see silver bath fixtures and a fist-sized hole where the drain should have been. Sweat poured from Manny's forehead as he clasped his hands together, expectant.

After a few moments, Manny rose and walked in a tight circle around the tub.

"Help me, Memaw," he cried. "Come on, now!"

Though I had no way of knowing then, poor Manny had been on his own from age sixteen, after his grandmother's heart quit cold where she sat in a rocking chair on the front porch, burnt out Chesterfield in her hand. Social services sniffed around the house like hungry dogs and came for Manny the day his memaw was cremated.

"My life just stopped. Until I came into your room that night and danced," he'd tell me often. Manny still remains the loneliest person I've ever met. I always considered the moment he brought me down from that attic room as our mutual rescue.

In the bathtub at the farmhouse, my body folded into the porcelain, obeying gravity's need to draw me deep into the earth, and a weak transmission surfaced. Muffled voices filtered through the static, briefly, and vanished into a crisp ocean of white noise. Manny moved my jaw from side to side, searching for the voices.

"Hold on," he said and stormed out.

The Girl sidled up to the vanity and rested her fingers delicately on the dial. Clenching my jaw, I ground my teeth, a nearly imperceptible effort, back and forth, just like the night we discovered the transmission. Back then we didn't know how to turn off the radio and so for hours old songs played with only intermittent talk from DJs. The Girl tossed and turned until eventually she left my field of vision for the first time in months. I grew so scared I cinched up involuntarily, clamping my jaw, and the radio stopped.

Now, at Manny's, after an hour of me grinding my teeth and her twisting the tuning nob, we found transmission.

::: *Change is gonna come* :::—The Girl shook her head, and turned the dial, skipping over any static— ::: *chchch* ::: *Down here at the super* ::: *chchch* :::

Manny didn't return until late that night. A pool of sweat and drool had formed on my chest from where my head lay still for so many hours.

"Not sure what to do, ma'am," he said. "Overreacted bringing you here."

The Girl paced. We were unhappy in Manny's bathtub, but we didn't like the attic back at Holy Oaks, either. I thought at Manny, told him not to give up. Told him to wait and see what The Girl and I had learned. And turning on the radio, a voice came.

::: *The north shore has seen quite a bit of lobster* ::: *chchch* ::: —No. No. The Girl changed stations. A doo-wop song came on— ::: *chchch* ::: *You better STOP!* ::: *chchch* ::: —Then a rock and roll song— ::: *I want to be* ::: *chchch* ::: *Here for you* ::: *chchch*— Then church— ::: *Salvation waits in places least expected. Listen for the call* :::

"You said it, girlie." Manny looked surprised by his own response. "Did you?"

::: *chchch* ::: *Be good, Baby* ::: *chchch* ::: *bloated fish* ::: *chchch* ::: *Ready for love* ::: *chchch* ::: *on home* ::: *chchch* :::

"You're about as fixed as they come," he said. "You gone haywire?"

Watching me intently, he sat down on the edge of the tub and searched my face.

That evening, Manny brought me up a plate of mashed potatoes and coleslaw. He wore a pair of purple dish gloves and a floral apron. At first, he didn't know how to feed me, and so the food leaked out onto my chin and onto my chest. He eventually got the hang of it, though.

"Used to feed the dogs heartworm pills this way," he said, rubbing my throat to help the food go down.

::: *chchch* ::: *Don Knots at the Grand Ol' Oprey* ::: *chchch* :::

"You ain't that much trouble, girlie," he said.

After dinner, Manny brought a little mattress up to the attic and laid down. We talked ourselves to sleep that night. Well, Manny did the talking. He told me about his memaw. About how his parents had gone on vacation to Mexico and got locked up for stealing a monkey from the zoo. It wasn't the theft, he said, that put them in a Mexican prison but that they'd loosed the little guy on the hotel manager. Manny had gone to prison, too.

"I was sent to the asylum to work, fresh out of county," he said. "I was tired of living. Didn't care what happened next but too proud to take my own life. So, I had some fun. Held up a gas station, even a bank. Wasn't until I ran a red light and kicked my old truck up to ninety that I served time. Six months. Came out a hungry man, a man with an appetite for living."

A week passed, and Manny hadn't bathed me in all that time, or changed me out of the gown I wore my last night at Holy Oaks.

"Not to embarrass you little lady, but we got to do something about your condition."

He looked so helpless. There was nothing I could do to relieve him of the chore ahead, but my nightie was covered in food, trails of urine, and grease from the back of his pickup. Manny put on a pair of dish gloves, removed my nightie, and tossed it in the garbage. "Got you something nicer," he said, and held up a gown thicker than burlap. "Belonged to Memaw."

Manny sponged water on me, and wetted my hair and body. Then he dug into me with soap, scrubbing away like I was gummed-up linoleum.

I tried to tell him to be gentle, but couldn't find the right words—::: *chchch* ::: *better specials* ::: *chchch* ::: *High concentrated* ::: *chchch* ::: *I'm on fire* ::: *chchch* :::

"Ain't ever seen a person so filthy."

He tried to roll me over so that he could clean my backside, but my body twisted as it caught the curves of the tub. Manny took a deep breath, and hoisted me over his shoulder, holding onto my waist with one hand as he scrubbed with the other. Electric pulses tingled my skin as he touched me. Hot all over even though the air had chilled. My wet body kept slipping down, but he'd heave me back up.

"Like a damn river fish, you are," he said as he flipped me around in front of him. But he lost his grip and I slipped from his arms. My face slammed hard against the porcelain tub.

We both heard the tinkling sound before we knew exactly what had happened. Manny righted me and pressed a towel against my bleeding cheek. A silver crown, cast in the shape of my back molar, sat in the bottom of the tub.

I still remember the day I got that crown. Daddy had taken me to the dentist after I'd refused to eat anything besides mashed potatoes for a week. The dentist had cupped a plastic mask over my face. Soon every little thing—the red bumps that edged the dentist's nose; the ceiling fan's slow *tick-tick-tick;* my daddy puffing his cheeks and making his eyes bug out—had me giggling.

"I knocked your tooth out," Manny said.

The Girl worked to get a radio signal, but there was only silence. Not even static. She at least could pull her hair, but me, I only waited for Manny to drag that old carpet-gown over my body. I concentrated on grinding my teeth but felt too panicked to control my slight jaw and clumsy eye movement. What a mess. The Girl spun the dial on that old transistor radio, and I threw up all over my newly bathed self.

Sweet Manny didn't flinch when he wiped the vomit away. And after he dressed me in his grandmother's gown, he said, "Been alone most my life. Got used to it." He moved loose strands of hair behind my ear, as if this kindness were natural to him. "S'posed it was natural," he said. "The silence, I mean."

It broke my heart to hear him say he enjoyed my company at the very moment I'd lost the transmissions. When I didn't respond, Manny grew agitated. "I tried to catch you."

Silence.

"Damn it all!" He stormed from the attic.

I could hear him rustling around downstairs. After a few moments, he came back with a tube of super glue.

"We gotta get that sucker back in!"

He tilted my head back, dabbed glue on the end of the silver filling, and opened my mouth wide, seeking the hole in my mouth. "Bingo!"

We waited.

"Come on now," Manny said. "Say something."

But no sound came.

The Girl and I stayed awake all night. She spent long stretches lying flat on her belly and picking lint off the rug. I stared up into the exposed ceiling beams.

Manny returned the next morning. Without even a "hello," he cradled me in his arms, and I knew for certain I'd be back at Holy Oaks by bedtime. But as he ran me out to the porch, I saw a TV antenna rigged to my wheelchair and knew right away what he intended. *Oh, Manny,* I thought, as he sat me down.

"I'd build a house on Everest to hear you yap again."

Manny chained my chair into the bed of his truck, and we drove. Bits of gummy glue drifted to the back of my throat from where he'd reset my filling. Black storm clouds swam across the sky. After the truck heaved and grunted over acres of Memaw's farmland, we reached the summit. It offers a beautiful view of the land, and every anniversary, we enjoy a picnic up on that hill. I bake a cake and Manny buys a six-pack of Coors and we listen to a portable FM radio. But on this day, large droplets of rain splattered sparsely over the field, fog obscuring the house. Manny slammed the truck brakes so hard my wheelchair toppled sideways. He hauled me down into the poverty grass. We waited for sound— nothing. The Girl and I worked at the radio. She tuned as I ground my jaw with those slight movements. Manny adjusted the antennae, but no transmission.

With my head leaned back into one of his paws, Manny opened my mouth to adjust the filling. Fat splatters ticked against the truck bed and then gave way to sheets of rain. Lightning. Thunder. Nothing could be seen, save water.

Frightened, her eyes wild with instinct, The Girl swung a wooden chair hard against the wall of her bedroom. I'd come to consider this space permanent, but the chair cracked the plaster and The Girl dug and scratched at the divot with her delicate fingers until a hole opened that was big enough for her to fit through. She saved me, I believe, and I don't know what she did behind the wall but her panic was the fighting kind. I felt as close to her then as when she'd first made herself known, cowering in the dark, sniffing the air for danger. I've never seen her again, but I think of her every time Manny and me dance or when I wear a dress that's a little risqué.

I hardly noticed Manny as he threw grass at the pelting sky, his frustration now an unstoppable tantrum. The wind tore across the field. And I recall thinking, just before my mind succumbed to a violent and beautiful white, about that missing deliveryman, the one the tornado plucked from his bread van and carried into oblivion. I wondered if he'd witnessed the funneling inside.

JUST LIKE *BLUE VELVET*

JUST LIKE *BLUE VELVET*

THE APARTMENT THAT Walter had until recently shared with his wife was on the fourth floor in a neighborhood where windows without plywood were a luxury. His spot had glass panes, linoleum floors, and bookshelves full of VHS tapes, DVDs, and a growing Blu-ray selection. He recalled how he used to take the stairs two at a time and how he'd always grab ahold of Marly, their bodies puzzling together snugly. After making love, they would heat up frozen pizza and drink beer and watch a film; Walter would obsess over the soundscape, diegetic or non-diegetic, loving the discordant and ambient noise more than the score.

He had fasted when he put on the first twenty pounds, and when that doubled, he drank prune juice until his innards clenched and he followed that up with a quinoa diet for three months. Nothing helped. First, his gut stretched against his shirt-buttons until he had to buy new clothes, and then his back fat slipped over his beltline. Marly gifted them both gym memberships for Christmas one year, twelve months of unlimited yoga lessons the next season, and hired a dietician the third. While she trimmed and her muscles toned, Walter bulged. He quit yoga, the gym, diet restrictions, and now, with one hand holding the banister while the other clutched a number two from McDonald's, he drew short breaths stair by stair.

Marly was no longer around to remind him of how quickly he'd given up, and so Walter often brought food home and ate while watching without sound whatever garbage the corporate annex had filmed that day. For five years, he created soundscapes for monolithic fast food chains, box stores, even the IRS. Once inside, he connected his work computer to the fifty-inch screen, removed burgers from the yellow wrappings, and stuffed a handful of fries into his mouth. He pressed play and watched as children hurled themselves into a bin of colorful balls. He'd been struggling with this one, McDonald's being a prominent nodule on the American psyche: he'd tried lifting the chainsaw buzz from *Massacre*, a consistent *eeeeeeeeeeee* beneath the footage, but the comparison between slaughter and consumerism felt cliché. He'd layered sounds from other commercials, old ones that no longer aired, like Domino's The Noid, so folks would crave pizza as opposed to burgers. It wasn't until he'd actually gone to Mickey D's on his way home that he'd had his *a-ha* moment—*Blue Velvet*: Denis Hopper huffing nitrous oxide while cutting away cloth from Isabella Rossellini's dress so near her vagina that Walter ached with the certainty (even after hundreds of views) that something far more violent was happening out of sight. In this way, he personalized the shit he was forced to design for corporate. He subliminally transmitted to millions of Americans the subtle influence of terror, lust, and jealousy, all through imperceptible sound.

It was odd, he thought, how the salt content in the burgers and fries changed his chewing habits; he was compelled to force a new bite before swallowing the last. He wasn't even hungry, but the taste triggered deprivation as if starved or dehydrated. The children on screen disappeared beneath the colorful surface and mothers smiled and cashiers handed over sacks of food and the clown waved. Walter was thirsty.

At the kitchen sink, he poured a glass of water. He hated the kitchen. Marly had painted the walls purple, Marly had burned the wooden handle off the skillet because she'd left the electric burner on all day, Marly had chipped the counter tile when she threw her boot at the cat, Marly had bled on the linoleum. A Marly Mosaic. The entire apartment was this way: the bedroom, of course, and the living room closet where she kept all of her clothes. He lingered on the closet, studied the accordion doors that were slightly ajar and there, sudden and frenzied, he saw a shift in shadow. This was the moment of tension when, as a sound designer, he'd lean into the score, upping the volume slightly, teasing out and manipulating the lower frequencies so they hummed horizontally through the moment, and when the volume peaked, the viewer was held in anticipation and unconsciously waited for the ear to be cleared of obstacles. Video was nothing without audio.

He grabbed a broom and approached the closet.

"Put that down," Marly said from behind the accordion doors. She stepped out of the closet casually, her hair in three-inch braids, wearing purple tights and an exercise bra.

"How many keys did you make?" he asked.

"I never agreed to leave *my* home." It was true. He'd broken up with her. And because she was flush with cash, he kept the rent-controlled apartment.

Marly approached him gently and took hold of his stomach in both hands. He couldn't remember what it felt like to be thin. Her touch, as it had for so long now, reminded him of all that he'd gained. "I miss you," she said. "All of you."

"Stop, please."

"You're such a swan. Stupid. Ugly. Swan."

"Marly."

"Shut up, Walter. I'm not here for you anyway. There is some shit going down. Remember last week when I came over to grab some clothes? I was talking to my secretary, per usual—"

Marly's "secretary" was a voice memo app she'd created for smartphones called "Dolly," in homage to Dolly Parton and her role in the movie *Nine to Five*. Walter remembered how after bad days, especially when she began working as the only woman at a Palo Alto incubator, Marly would put on *Nine to Five* and flip through to her favorite scenes, and after she felt "Bad like Dolly," she'd go for a run and then shower and then she'd talk with Walter, but never before this routine had finished.

"Please, Marly."

"You are not hearing me. Last night I'm doing yoga and listening back over my notes for the week, and right in the middle of tree pose I hear, like, a woman screaming. I think it's outside my spot, but when I cut the sound: nothing. I'm like, forget it, and press play. The scream happens again. Don't believe me? Listen for yourself, Wal."

"I don't want to—this hurts me, you dressed like an aerobics instructor."

"It's my disguise, baby. To throw off the fools that snatched 2-C."

"Gloria in 2-C?"

"That's what I'm trying to tell you. I was in tree pose and then I hear a scream. It's not coming from Meadow Lawn but from the recording. I put on headphones. All I can hear is mumbling and then the scream. I know it's her because I made out one word—'Pendejada!'"

"Pendejada?"

"Don't act stupid. You know: *Todo es una pendejada.*"

Walter knew what she meant. In private, they called their neighbor from 2-C Gloria Pendejada. She handed him a thumb drive.

"Just listen," she said. "I'll come by your work tomorrow."

He was powerless. Two years had passed since he'd been able to hold an erection; as soon as his shirt and pants came off, he withered at the sight of his own body. He took the flash drive, already imagining the softness of sleep once he'd polished off a bottle of wine from the case he bought each week.

"None of this explains why you are hiding in the closet."

"To listen out for Gloria Pendejada or for the bastard who kidnapped her."

After Marly left, Walter walked across the hall and knocked on Belinda's door. To most, Belinda was known simply as Super. There was nothing quiet or calm about Super Belinda, and as Walter waited, sounds erupted from inside—clashing metal, wood scooting against wood, TV rising in volume from normal to supersonic to silent, stomps and curses. The door opened. Belinda, in a silk kimono, her head cocked to the side, hand on her hip, and a smear of lipstick rising upward from her mouth, stared at Walter without speaking. All communication that could be done through her eyes was conveyed in a slow study of his person.

"Marly thinks something happened to Gloria in 2-C."

"How is Marly gonna know anything about my building now that she's taken her fancy ass over to Meadow Lawn?"

From inside her apartment, Bird called, "Tell him to leave us alone. I didn't come over to freeze to death in this cold-ass house. Turn on the heat—" Bird's rant continued as Belinda pulled the door closed. Bird was there nightly but he always claimed to live elsewhere, threatening to go back there so loudly that some mornings Walter feared he might wake up and find Bird gone. The apartment without Bird was as hard to imagine as the complex without Gloria Pendejada.

"Will you check?"

Belinda did not blink. Walter hated this motionless stare. He interacted with the world through sound while Belinda and Marly were all sight. She did not break her gaze as she told Bird to shut up and bring the building keys from her nightstand drawer. He grumbled but did not argue. Bird stood in the doorway wearing one of Belinda's kimonos.

"I'm gonna get you for this, Walter. Bringing me out of bed after the premiere of *Curb Your Enthusiasm* has already started."

"The new season? I've got a bootleg of all the episodes."

Bird looked to Belinda, then to Walter and nodded. "Don't come back without my show."

Every apartment was identical, and so Walter could easily imagine Bird's route from entrance to bedroom, and he thought about Gloria and he also thought about Roger and Harriet who lived below him and everyone else in the complex. He thought about this shared symmetry, about how environment shaped humans, and he wondered if over the years they had all formed a clan-like bond based on this navigation of space even though they never spoke with one another. Belinda knocked, and when there was no answer, she slid the key into Gloria Pendejada's lock. Walter was struck by a sudden fear that something really *had* happened to her, and the undigested McDonald's burger rose up and caught in his throat, and he belched.

"Gloria, honey? I'm coming in. If you're natural, then please put on some clothes."

It seemed to Walter that when the anticipated *Ay Pendejada* did not follow Belinda's request, she stiffened. Gloria was the resident recluse, living alone and receiving her goods through the mail or delivery services. Belinda did not turn the key.

"I can't do it, Walter."

He unlatched the door to reveal a dark, spotless apartment. The windows were covered in blackout curtains and there were no bulbs in the overhead lights. Walter stepped softly throughout the room, honestly afraid he might trip over Gloria's body, and clicked on the lamps within reach. As the living room warmed with lamplight tampered by canvas shades, he saw the perfection in which Gloria lived. There was no dust; every surface shone with polish. The rug did not only look vacuumed but washed, and the linoleum floor beneath, waxed. Gloria had meticulously arranged gilded picture frames and porcelain hound dogs on her mantel; even the magnets on her fridge were precisely spaced. Why Walter expected the opposite was an outcome of his own prejudices. Gloria always seemed fearful and mean-spirited, and so, he imagined squalor to match what he gleaned of her personality. This room complicated his vision of Gloria.

Belinda did not speak as she made her way into the bedroom and returned with a more relaxed posture than when she'd entered. For a moment, he did not know what to do with his body and he moved from counter to table, pacing the same path he'd made in his own apartment over the weeks since Marly had moved out, afraid that if he stopped, he might show Belinda his ballooning concern. He recalled other experiences in life when he felt similar fear and anticipation, this horrible waiting: his father calling to say his mother had left him to pursue a career in commercial fishing, Marly staying out until three in the morning with Joe from accounting, and the months it took before hearing back from Stanford.

"Stop pacing, Walter."

He followed Belinda's stare. At the edge of the immaculately kept rug, a human finger blended perfectly with the yellowish linoleum beneath. There was no blood, and the cut seemed to be clean and straight with two knuckles and the fingernail intact.

That squirrely motherfucker Butter was on security at Walter's office when Marly arrived at the studio. Butter was white with blond cornrows, he slouched, and his uniform fell off his ass. Marly was the child of Nigerian immigrants. Her brother, a pretty-boy with a master's degree in chemistry from Yale was working at Chick-fil-A because of a possession-with-intent-to-sell charge after a San Jose pig found a blunt in his briefcase. Butter reeked of weed *right now,* and his narrow ass was a cop.

"You get finer every time I see you, girl."

"Sign me in, Butter. Sign me in, and don't you dare look anywhere but my face."

"Dang. I'm just tryin'a compliment you."

She found Walter in his throne room, alone, surrounded by monitors set to pause. The scene was from an embarrassing slasher flick—*Cutter Ridge: Part Three*—but this one had more money because the producer was a twenty-four-year-old start-up guru who made a killing off a scratch-and-sniff app that informed each participant what fruit they were. He'd pulled in a once-heavy-hitting director who'd been socially dead for two decades after he'd been arrested trying to bring back a human skeleton from China. Walter was just now—three years since the first shoot—doing sound for a film that should have had a sixteen-month turnaround. Marly had never told Walter that she blamed this film for their problems. Walter had vision. If anyone gave a shit, he could be on the forefront of sound-art, like James Turrell had done for light. But the moment he began working B-Horror flicks and commercials something changed. His hours were the same; he still had plenty of time to work on his own art after he'd finished up with corporate, but it was like he'd given up on life the moment he'd signed the contract. It *had been* his fault, though, always complaining about his life, his weight, his job, and at the same time growing and not trying at all. He wasn't even fat, she thought, just a corn-fed white boy from Iowa who turned forty without going for a jog once in his life. The more he withdrew into his depression, the more she wanted to, like, *inspire* self-care. As she trimmed up, she thought this would urge him to get his muscle on, but instead, he dumped her ass.

"Wal? Walter!"

When he still didn't respond, she walked closer and set her laptop down next to his Big Gulp of Mountain Dew. Once, when they were sophomores in college, she teased him for his tastes—"That's so nasty! Look at the color"—and he'd said, with such sincerity, "It's the soda my family drinks."

"Jesus, Marly!"

"Do you have a dongle? Plug me in."

"I've got it pulled up already. You will not fucking believe my night! You were right. Gloria is gone, like, disappeared. Belinda and I found a fucking finger. Do you know what the cops said? They said they'd take it to the coroner, but missing persons are rarely found, so don't hope to see her anytime soon. They just bagged the finger and walked out, didn't even take a statement after I told them what you told me. I couldn't sleep. I came here."

Marly saw her file bootlegged from Dolly and labeled GLORIA-MEMO on the screen. The sound graph had been stretched so wide all differentiation between frequencies was combined into a wide block. Walter pressed play and voices came through warbling as if underwater, but clear enough to hear what Gloria said to a man that called her Grandma. "I told you, mijo. I don't want to leave. This is my home. I'm not crippled or crazy besides." There was a loud crash as if mijo had thrown something metallic against the wall and he said "You can't live alone anymore, Grandma." What followed was scratchy from the volume of Gloria's voice, but one word had been loud enough for Marly to hear over her dictation to Dolly—"Pendejada!" The door slammed, and then nothing but street traffic, and a car starting outside of the apartment's stoop. Walter and Marly exchanged looks that communicated so many different things at once, a conspiratorial exchange full of delight and guilt for this shared pleasure, and if Marly were to read Walter's smile correctly, love. He loved her; she knew it. She didn't want to push though, didn't want him to crawl inside of his shell, and so she was the first to avert her gaze, to study the red needle that purred across the sound graph.

They decided not to tell Belinda about what they heard on the Dolly memo, she had enough on her plate, and the police were out. Marly hated cops, *hated* how they looked at her brother, glaring, how they looked her, lustful. Besides, OPD had already made it clear they wanted nothing to do with Gloria.

Instead, Marly talked sweetly to Butter until he agreed to meet her at Roscoe's Diner around the corner from the apartment. She said he must come wearing a clean and pressed security uniform with the utility belt. Butter, of course, had no idea what he was summoned for, and Marly did not dissuade his juvenile fantasies.

Walter and Marly took the corner booth nearest the front door so they could see when Butter approached. It was only the day after discovering mijo's involvement in Gloria's disappearance, but they both felt too much time had lapsed considering Marly had made the recording a week before.

"It's just like *Blue Velvet*," Marly said.

"It's funny you say that because just before I caught you hiding in the closet, I was thinking of that scene with Hopper and the scissors, you know, while Kyle MacLachlan hid in the closet. Then *the finger*. I mean it was a finger not an ear, but, like, what are the odds!"

"You said it was a strange world, and you're the strangest part of it," Marly quoted from the diner scene with Laura Dern and MacLachlan.

"There's Butter," Walter said.

Marly turned and caught Butter checking himself in the glass: tucking down a blond cornrow that had unhitched in the wind, his thin hair rejecting the binds and fraying. He pulled his blue security pants down, untucking his shirt so that the ends barely covered a pair of blue-and-white striped boxer briefs. Marly winked at Walter and sashayed from the booth, meeting Butter at the entrance, taking hold of his arm. It was all so fake. Marly's kindness and flirtation was extravagant and overacted, but Walter felt a rage heat up inside of him at the sight of Marly touching Butter. Butter grabbed her waist as Marly maneuvered him to the booth.

"Yo, love, what's Snuffleupagus doing here? I thought this was, like, about you and me."

Marly told Butter that he looked good. "I need your help with something," she said.

The server came to their table, and Walter watched as Butter pulled away from Marly, and he saw in Butter's expression that he knew he was being used but was weighing the odds of whether or not Marly might actually fuck him. Walter recognized this look, embarrassed but hopeful; he'd seen the expression on so many men over the years with Marly. It was like they couldn't help but want her even when she was cruel and disgusted by their advances. This used to make Walter proud, knowing that his wife could incite such self-immolating desire in others. But watching her with Butter now that they were no longer together, now that they did not owe each other monogamy, he feared Butter's fantasy might become his nightmare. After Butter ordered a BLT and Marly ordered a Caesar salad, the server looked at Walter, pen poised as if she meant to write fast and hard. He hesitated though he was starving, and said, "I'm not hungry. Coffee is fine." He hated the look the server gave him, a quick widening of the eyes before an attempt to clear her face of thought and feeling.

"We need you to act like a cop," Marly said. "Like, pull your pants up, tuck in your shirt and wear the utility belt with the baton and taser. The whole shebang, baby! You know I can't contain myself around a man in uniform. Ain't that right, Walter? Don't I love a cop?"

Walter sipped his coffee.

Butter shifted in his seat, nervously tidied creases from his ironed shirt; Walter saw then that all his bravado was performance. If he ever got Marly alone and naked, he'd pop off before dropping those Calvin's. Butter was a boy, and a stupid one at that, but if Walter could just coach him into sticking to the script, the plan might work.

"All you have to do is come to my complex and ring the superintendent's bell and say you are a cop that has to follow up on the crime scene in 2-C. That's it. Don't say anything else. If Belinda asks you a question, just say *police business*," Walter said. "As soon as I hear y'all enter 2-C, I'll call Belinda back upstairs. Marly will swoop in and swap Gloria's key for a fake. Jog upstairs and hand off Belinda's set and say *all done*."

"Why y'all need to break into this apartment? I'm not tryn'a go to jail over some bullshit. And does this uniform say 'Police Department'? No. It says, 'Public Security.'"

"You're a rookie, not yet on the job. Still in training, but you get high marks, and the squad is spread thin, overworked," Walter said. "Sergeant sent you because he sees potential. Got it? You need to do a follow-up inspection. But the real reason this will work is because Belinda is worried, and she wants to believe the cops care about people like Gloria."

Walter left before their food came. He stood at the entrance to the diner and watched as Marly ran her fingers down the flaking scalp between Butter's cornrows, watched as Butter tossed his arm over her shoulder, his hand swaying an inch in front of Marly's left breast. *Damn Marly if she thought he was going to get jealous over Butter, and damn Butter if he thought he had a chance with his wife,* Walter thought. But back in his apartment, he paced and waited for Butter's knock on Belinda's door. As he unscrewed the drain-pipe below his kitchen sink, he let his imagination flow unchecked. Butter had driven his 1970 Buick Skylark to the diner, he knew, and they could have parked anywhere for a quick fuck, or worse, Marly was blowing Butter right now. He was starved after skipping lunch at the diner, and he ached with the false image of Marly together with Butter in Butter's stupidly inefficient Skylark, and he could not push the story aside, but instead, he edited the footage, added conversation as he drove them into an alley and—

There was a knock on Belinda's door across the hall. Through the eyehole, Walter saw Butter shuffling uncomfortably in his uniform that now, thankfully, was belted above his waist, his shirt buttoned and tucked. Butter's hair surprised Walter the most; all the rows had been unbraided and his soft blond hair was waxed and combed with a side-part. Even from behind his door, Walter could smell the acrid tang, like burning plastic, of hair straightener, and he knew then that what had taken them so long was that Marly had persuaded this makeover and once the cornrows were freed, they had to deal with the crinkly hair. He knew the chemical burned, and for a moment, he felt sorry for Butter. Belinda answered the door, and Butter, surprisingly, did not stammer. He delivered his lines with what Walter thought was an authentic mixture of authority and unease, just like a cop, and soon Butter and Belinda were downstairs and Walter listened for echoing voices and 2-C's unlatched door, and when he was certain Butter and Belinda were inside Gloria's apartment, he called after Belinda in what he hoped sounded like a frantic voice.

"There's water exploding from my sink. Belinda!"

"Hang on! Don't touch a thing," Belinda said and Walter jogged to his kitchen sink, opened the cabinet door, and turned on the faucet. Water sprayed in all directions from the unmoored drainpipe, and when Belinda stepped in, she cursed him, told him to turn off the damn tap before he drowned the whole complex.

"You said don't touch anything."

"Don't act a fool, Walter. You know this drainpipe came loose. Bet your lazy ass knows all you got to do is screw it back on, like so, too."

He should have thought of a different means to bring Belinda upstairs. It took her all of two seconds to connect the elbow back in place, and then she wiped down the surface inside his cabinet and the floor beneath not because she had to, he would have cleaned up, but because she couldn't help it; each apartment was as much hers as it was anyone's. She'd been there the longest, and as far as Walter knew, she had always been Super. She was done now, and Butter had yet to jog upstairs with the keys and say *all done.*

"Bird still want a copy of *Curb Your Enthusiasm*?"

"Lord, yes! Thanks for reminding me. He has been complaining nonstop since you showed up the other night. Says he can't follow the jokes because he missed the inciting incident. I said, '*Inciting incident?* What you been into lately that you even think those words?' And you know he pulled out a book called *The Screenwriter's Guide to Hollywood.* Says he's gonna write for TV. Says all the crazy shit that goes on here is enough material to last twenty seasons. I said, 'Cash your check, then, and write yourself a ticket to Hollywood.'"

The whole time Belinda was talking, Walter fumbled with his computer, pretending the files were taking a long time to burn when in fact he'd already made copies for Bird. He opened a Word doc, tapped at random on his laptop keyboard, and apologized for how slow his computer was running.

"Excuse me, ma'am," Butter said from the doorway. "Here's your keys, and I locked back up downstairs."

Belinda thanked Butter. "At least someone around here knows how to act right." She eyed Walter in that way of hers that made him feel stupid and small but loved all at once, and Walter handed her the discs to give to Bird, and Butter said goodbye, and Belinda said goodbye, and Walter closed the door.

When he called her, Marly picked up on the first ring. "I've got the key," she said. "See you tonight."

Marly was fifteen minutes late. Walter sat in his recliner but felt too complacent, and so he walked to the kitchen, wiped the stove and sides of the refrigerator with a rag and drank tap water. He stood, as men do in films, with one hand rested on the counter, and studied the glass as if it were filled with scotch. His counter was shorter than most and the ceiling was dropped and so the angle of his lean felt awkward and hurt his shoulder. From his cabinet, he pulled out a wine bottle, twisted the top, and drank. Two gulps in, and he focused on the fuzzy warmth rather than the cool tremors that tickled his loins. Marly had looked good today. Her act was hilarious, and they were drumming up the truth behind Gloria's disappearance as a team.

A knock. From across the hall, though, and Walter sank against the counter and checked his watch wondering where Marly was until he heard her voice in conversation with Belinda.

"Honey! Are you back? You know, Walter has been a moping mess since you left."

"We're just having dinner. I'm still exiled."

Walter watched from the eyehole as the two women spoke. Marly wore a dress, black with tropical birds in blues and oranges that had once been his favorite. She'd gone to the salon and gotten dreadlock extensions that were now wrapped in a large hive atop her head. Walter knew this was an expensive and arduous undertaking, and he hesitated thinking the work had been done for him;

Marly often changed her hair. Belinda, too, was dressed up in gray slacks, boots, and a gray blazer-blouse combo. Marly made sure to compliment Belinda, something Walter would have never done because those sorts of interactions always seemed to continue into long explanations of where the clothes had come from and why they were bought and why they were worn at this very moment.

"Bird's got this seminar over in Emeryville. Thinks he's gonna write a TV show."

"You read my script, Lin! It's damn good. You know it's good, too." Bird yelled.

"Oh, wow," Marly said, barely hiding her initial shock at the idea.

"Hmm-hmm. Gonna be about how Gloria was snatched by the mob and about he, or the *protagonist,* as that fool keeps correcting, an out of work janitor, turns detective and solves the crime. Says he's got three seasons outlined."

Marly laughed. Her nervous laugh, Walter knew; the laugh that came when she was anxious or scared and often did not stop until she'd calmed down. He watched her briefly, hoping she would contain the laughing, but she kept stammering "I'm sor—" never getting the full apology out.

"You're here, Marly. Come in."

He was still holding the bottle of wine, half full now, and both women eyed him suspiciously. Marly's laugh slid into little coughs. Walter ushered Marly to safety. When the door was latched, she slid against his body, wrapping her arms around his waist, her face buried in his neck. She mumbled apologies over offending Bird, about how Belinda would never forgive her, and her breath was hot and damp below his ear. "Can you believe Bird's story idea? What are we doing, Wal?"

"Looking for clues, I guess. I mean, wasn't Gloria one of our own?"

"Did you ever talk to the woman? I think I only saw her once."

When Marly pulled away, Walter instinctively tightened his grip, and she snuggled closer. Her hand slipped below the fold of belly at his waistband, and she explored him as if this part of his body was a fine fabric. Walter closed his eyes, willing himself to simply feel her touch without thinking too much about his body.

"Your skin is so soft, Walter."

"Marly."

"I liked how jealous you got today, all pissy and not eating lunch. Butter didn't have a clue, but I saw you thought I was jocking him for real. I saw you get fired up, and I knew—"

"Marly. Wait—"

"Come off it with your sour-ass, and let me love you a little."

"No, Marly. Look." He pulled away from her. The crotch of his sweatpants stretched against his erection, the first full erection he'd had in over a year. She clapped for him, as if his erection was a magic trick, and he kissed her full on the mouth. At first, she returned the kiss, each letting tongues investigate these familiar reaches; her lips full and wet. She nibbled, and he held her tighter, pressing into her. Marly stopped.

"Not so fast," she said. "I'm not going to lay down for you that easy, not after all you put me through these past few years."

Walter came to his senses: what was he thinking? "You're right," he said. "I just got excited."

Walter still held the bottle of wine in one hand, and he handed it to Marly. She drank from the bottle as he had before her, and they both sat at the kitchen table, passing swigs back and forth. There was so much to talk about, so many hurt feelings to parse, so many injustices small and large, but there was no point in going over it all again because they'd already hashed out every difficult thing.

They were lucky that Belinda and Bird would be out for the night and they waited, listening for footsteps, talking low about Gloria and this mijo who was cold enough to kidnap his grand-mother. Why? That's what it came down to now, the reason Marly was going to unlock 2-C and snoop around for evidence. She did not know what she hoped to find; there was a missing woman and a found finger and a cynical police department. The likelihood of her turning over strong facts that might lead to Gloria Pendejada was slim, but they had to try. Didn't they have to try?

Marly went straight for the cabinets and desk once inside Gloria's apartment, anything with drawers, searching for money info. If she knew family, this mijo was after Gloria's bank account, apartment, or both. Gloria wasn't old-*old,* but definitely past seventy and could afford to pay rent and bills without ever leaving the house, so she was either flush with inheritance or on a fixed income. In Marly's mind, all grandmothers thought alike, and she was right to seek the bill drawer, just like at her mimi's house, just like at Walter's gramma's house, because there, in the kitchen cabinet, was a file folder where Gloria had kept every bill and financial transaction going back ten years at least. She was organized too, with colored tags delineating each year with other colored tags delineating the source: SSI, Medicare, electricity, and even a section for rent stubs. Marly had never thought to ask Belinda for a receipt, but Gloria had, and her Mimi would have too. Their generation was more suspicious of authority, having come up in the Depression, and they knew how quick the bottom could fall out for the poor when folks played with your money. Marly found motive easily enough. Gloria received SSI checks via direct deposit, and Marly didn't find a checkbook or purse. Either mijo let Gloria take these financials with her, or he now controlled her fixed income.

If Gloria *was* like Mimi, there would also be a drawer full of correspondences: birthday cards, Christmas cards, letters from relatives describing hip surgeries and braces and private schools or expulsions from public schools. She found this drawer and nearly wept when she read over three—*only three!*—pieces of mail set aside. One was from her daughter dated fifteen years ago: Chester, her grandson by the sound of it, had entered magician's school in San Francisco. She'd divorced her husband, Chester's father, and planned to move to The Bay from Chicago to be near Gloria and her son. The second was from Chester, asking for money. The third was from Chester, saying that his mother had died in her sleep. Chester was mijo, that was clear, and Gloria's daughter had died more than a decade before and no one, not even Chester had written her since. Perhaps he called and visited 2-C, and no one in the building knew? Marly hoped he'd been kind to Gloria before shuffling her out of her home.

Marly heard the foyer door open, and her intuition told her to hide. This response was simply survival instinct but then again, she knew the cadence of each resident's footsteps, how their keys jingled, how they climbed the stairs. No one new had rented since she and Walter moved in ten years before. They were family by proximity, melded together by this sharing of space. And the footsteps she now heard, two pairs, she did not recognize. They were quick-tempered and hustled in earnest to 2-C, and Marly, not knowing what else to do, hid in the closet behind the accordion doors identical to her own, or, now, identical to Walter's.

Through the accordion slats of the closet door, Marly watched the couple enter; they looked more like a pair of strangers strolling close together by chance rather than lovers. Chester —because it had to be mijo—was dressed in athletic shorts that drooped below the knees and a Raiders T-shirt at least three sizes too big for his wiry frame. He was extra small: no taller than five-three and maxing out, if Marly guessed, at 110 pounds. To make up for his stature, he adorned his wrists and neck with gold. He had a Rolex on one wrist and tattooed sleeves growing up both arms. The woman was tall and muscular with a firm ass and a bra that pushed her breasts up and out. Marly studied this woman through the thin slats of the accordion doors; her legs were long and her eyes were large and a strange blend of hazel and gold, like alligator eyes, and she wore Louboutin heels and held a Balenciaga Ville purse in the crook of her elbow. An olive blouse, vintage silk, had gold clasps that buckled up her spine.

"I'll get the suitcases," Chester said.

The woman didn't respond. She studied the apartment with cold judgment, touched surfaces at random and said *ewww* when she turned her gaze on the floral-printed couch with a hand-woven afghan draped across the back. Her phone rang, and she tapped a microscopic earpiece twice and spoke into the room. "You won't believe this dump where Chess has brought me! Mama, it is all kinds of old people in here—I *know*. I told him. He says it's temporary—I *know*. It's better than where he was living with Ramon and Matthew, always practicing and none of them funny or cute. Not like Chess—Mama, you shut your mouth. You know my man is cute! Like a little Houdini—I know. His agent said he's got talent, gonna be on the national circuit—Shut up about you heard this all before."

Chester returned carrying three suitcases, panting. The woman, with a wide sweep of one finger, appraised the entire apartment. "All this has got to go," she said to Chester. "We need new furniture; take them blinds down."

Chester followed her finger with what seemed like his whole body, swiveling from boudoir to couch and coffee table, to the eating table in the kitchen and the curtains covering the windows. All the while, he watched and waited with a devoted, stupid smile.

"You should see this place, Mama. It's like Granma's house but more old—I know. I know. We'll get you up here as soon as Chess buys some new furniture. I can't have my mama coming to California and staying in a mausoleum. Shoot. After all that time in Missouri, you gonna get the full West Coast treatment."

Chester leaned toward the woman for a kiss before whispering, "Be right back," but she turned her lips away and he caught the lapel of her blouse. The woman's eyes were unfocused as she listened to the mother in Missouri. "I *know*," she said, unperturbed by Chester's advances and walked down the hall and into the bedroom.

This was Marly's chance to run, but she wasn't brave enough. All of her insides jittered with the impulse to flee, flee now, but her mind rebuffed the body, and she stayed standing in the closet. She'd hoped they would leave once the suitcases were all inside, perhaps go out for dinner or dancing. That was not the case. Chester returned carrying three more suitcases, and the woman continued to talk to her mother on the phone. He tried twice more to engage her attentions but was ignored—no, that's not quite right, Marly thought, it was like he was so removed from this woman's consciousness that he was too insignificant to even overlook. He did not seem to mind or even notice, but instead, he whistled and brought a medium-sized satchel to the bathroom where Marly had a direct view from her station in the closet. She watched through the accordion slats as he piled many small jars onto the toilet and sink and with methodical patience began to apply a thick layer of foundation to his forehead, cheeks, and jaw. Occasionally, when he leaned into the mirror to inspect his work, Marly made out his face and he looked content, happy even, as he smudged mascara below his eyes. For a moment, Marly felt sorry for Chester, even though she knew what he'd done to Gloria; she felt sorry for him because he had no idea to what extent his life with this woman was too good to be true.

The woman, as if sensing Marly's thoughts, walked cautiously toward the closet. "Just a second, Mama," she said. And her scream, when she caught sight of Marly hiding behind the accordion doors was multitudinous, as if a forest existed within her. Chester jogged to the front room, his face half-covered in rouge and eyeliner, asking again and again, "Dorothy, what's wrong?" as if he had caught hiccups and couldn't stop the words from coming even when he saw Marly standing in her black dress, her dreads high above her head. Marly mumbled an apology and ran away, fumbling with the doorknob before leaping down the foyer steps two at a time and onto the street beyond the entrance.

Walter heard the woman's scream from his apartment, and he frantically dialed Marly again and again, but he could not get her on the phone for another hour. By then, Belinda and Bird had already returned home and found lights on in Gloria's apartment. Walter eased his door open and listened to the heated exchange between the mijo and Super. It was painful, Walter later thought, how obvious his lies were when he told Belinda that Gloria had fallen and called an ambulance, and the hospital contacted him, her only relative, and that she was now living—temporarily, he added—in assisted living until she recovered, and that he and his novia were staying at Gloria's until she returned. Walter could visualize Belinda's cold appraisal of his person before she and Bird turned away and walked heavily upstairs. It was then, without consulting Marly, Walter decided to tell Belinda and Bird what he knew about Gloria. When they reached the top of the stairs, he whispered the two inside of his apartment, and in what felt embarrassing and melodramatic, but necessary to avoid suspicion, he told them to wait fifteen minutes and then drive to Marly's condo on Meadow Lawn. He would follow.

Marly was shaken, though she pretended bravado as she set out two bottles of wine and four glasses on the kitchen table. "Y'all need to listen to something," she said.

Walter pulled up the doctored Dolly file on his laptop and played the garbled, but clear interaction between Chester and Gloria Pendejada in 2-C. When the recording had finished, Belinda was quiet and Bird said, "I told you something noir was going down!"

"Something noir, all right," Belinda said. "I'm gonna *noir* that twerp all the way down to Jack London and kick his ass into the bay after messing with one of mine—" Belinda paused what was about to become an epic rant and looked inquisitively at Walter. "Do you think he cut the finger off his own grandma?"

Walter did not know, hadn't seen the man in person. Marly had, and after a pause, she said, "No. But Dorothy could've."

"There is no other voice on the recording, just Gloria and Chester," Bird said. "You think she was in the car or something?

And why bring the finger back inside so as to rile suspicion when he is trying to play it all off as if they're innocent?"

"While y'all play *protagonist,*" Belinda said, "and talk about *noir* this and *noir* that, I'm calling a tenant meeting. Cops don't care about us, so we'll find justice my way."

With that assurance, a silent and aggressive campaign had been struck against the enemy tenants of 2-C. First, Belinda drained all Freon from the wall-mounted air conditioner so that the room filled with hot, moist air, and when Chester approached her, she told him that tenants paid to replace Freon, and that she wasn't in charge of keeping folks comfortable, and when Chester complained that the windows were all sealed Belinda told him he had a choice between getting robbed or buying a fan. Second, Harriet in 3-D, after years of begging Belinda to host a girl scout bake-off in her apartment, was offered the opportunity to move troop meetings to the complex permanently, and so one night a week, from 6:00 until 8:00 p.m., the complex resounded with eleven preteen girls who practiced jump rope, square dancing, baking, and even banjo. And finally, Johnson—the owner of a neighborhood reptile emporium—recommended they plan to release rats on Wednesday when the weather was supposed to spike to 110 and the Brownies were scheduled to practice skits for the upcoming city-wide talent show. Nightly, the sharp and angry protests of Chester's girlfriend could be heard throughout the complex, and they all relished the assault, waiting patiently for the couple to give up and return Gloria back home.

And while the apartment complex fought in Belinda's dirty war, Walter and Marly continued their search for Gloria Pendejada. Walter had conversations with Chester and his girlfriend, making small talk about Gloria's alleged health and how the hospital was treating her—*which hospital did you say?*—but the couple made it clear they did not want to talk about Gloria. Neither Marly nor Walter had any clue where to look. They could not break into the apartment after Marly's previous discovery, and so most nights, Walter visited her condo, and they drank wine and talked.

"You can move here, you know. Quit your job. We could go anywhere," Marly said. "Maybe it's just what we need, movement."

Walter had not gone to work in six days, not since the war against 2-C began. Each morning he awoke, he felt clear and fluid, suddenly aching with the certainty that, like Atlas, he'd been tricked into the holding his world aloft. "You're right. I could get addicted to this weightlessness, but I have to work."

"You know how much my bonus was—*my bonus*—half your yearly salary. Live off me. I'm more husband than you could ever be."

"Remember that sound installation I put up during my residency at SFMoMA after completing my MFA?"

This was the work Walter was most proud of completing. He and Marly had hung black canvas in narrow aisles throughout a large room with high ceilings. People walked through the aisles while the speakers, set up every few feet, played noises that intensified or leveled off depending on heat censors. He had intentionally left the work lights on overhead but had no lights on through the maze so the walkers knew that they were surrounded by an abundance of square footage. At the end, monitors played on a five-minute delay so that the people, as they exited, were forced to view their procession: amusement turned to doubt turned to terror. A fucking *LA Times* reporter called it "melodramatic," called Walter "a boy playing haunted house when a *true artist* could've used that space to challenge perceptions."

"Then you took the sound job on the slasher-flick? I've never added those two events together before, but I see. You forgot *The New York Times*. They agreed about the haunted house business, but they also called you a name to look out for—"

"The MoMA didn't renew my residency, did they?"

"Walter—"

"Forget about it, Marly. I'm just whining. I make good money and can—"

"No, not that, Walter. Let's drop microphones into 2-C. Maybe they will slip up and mention Gloria?"

When Walter returned home that night, he found flyers rubber banded to each doorknob on his way upstairs: an advertisement for The Amazing Professor Chess and His Electric Companion two weeks from Friday. There was a photo of the woman in 2-C, her hair levitating around her face in blue streaks of lightning. There was a date, and the venue was close by, a not-so-small playhouse near the water. He texted Marly a photo, and she responded immediately, "We are going to that shit!" Even after polishing off a new bottle of wine on top of what he'd already had at Marly's, Walter couldn't sleep. He honestly didn't like the idea of bugging 2-C, but this had to end somewhere, and they had no other leads.

Walter drove to his office and grabbed a couple wireless lapel mics that he planned to drop somewhere in the living room once the couple was out together. He'd use the spare key Marly stole with Butter's help. He was lucky, or they were unlucky, because he saw Chester and His Electric Companion leaving the complex as he walked up. They exchanged hellos, and Chester asked if Walter thought he might come to the show.

"Planning on it," Walter said.

"My man is a genius," Dorothy said.

He waited in the darkened foyer until he saw Chester's car pull away, and then he unlocked 2-C. Nothing had changed inside of Gloria's apartment. There was a new smell on top of the old, and clothes were scattered about, and there was dust and dirty dishes, but it was still set up with all of Gloria's furniture and mementos, and it was hot. Walter dropped one mic in an ornate vase with plastic daisies and another behind the couch. He would eat the cost, buy new ones the next time they were needed on set. What bothered Walter, as he linked a lithium recorder to receive transmissions from the two mics, was that he knew that he would not want anyone to hear how he talked with Marly when alone. He wasn't concerned about recording sex, but about the bickering and petty squabbles, the complaints and small aggressions, all of those little moments that add up—when one is tired and says, "will you give me some space," or, when one has done a poor job with the dishes and the other says something hasty, like, "you always short-change things"—all of those minor cruelties that seep into a life. Walter pressed the record/trigger function on the pick-up and stuck it inside of his own mailbox. It was close to three in the morning, and he fell asleep at once, depleted: sad for Chester, sad for Gloria, and sad for Marly.

In the end, he couldn't bring himself to listen to the recordings, and so Marly took over the task of combing through hours of boring, everyday life of another couple and then, at night over wine, she'd recount to Walter all that she'd heard.

Marly usually stopped by the complex at 6:00 a.m. before heading off to work. She unlocked Walter's mailbox and downloaded the files from the lithium pick-up. Not even Belinda was awake that early, and after getting a handle on Chester and Dorothy's schedule, she knew for certain there was no chance of scaring up another encounter.

Dorothy rarely wanted to have sex because it might interfere with various skin creams and make-up or wrinkle her clothes. Dorothy and Chester both slept a good part of the day and stayed up late at night; Dorothy talked on the phone constantly, rarely making time for Chester. Marly kept tabs on Belinda's war through Dorothy's complaints to her mother in Missouri, and the campaign was effectively making the apartment inhospitable to both. There were also kind moments between the two: Dorothy hourly reassured Chester of his brilliance. Throughout this juicy invasion of privacy, there was not a single mention of Gloria.

Then came the rats, scared albino snake-food that cowered in the cage and did not run when Johnson and Belinda set them free in 2-C: a *coup de grâce* that drove Chester to buy at least three Havahart traps and set them up throughout 2-C. Dorothy left and flew to Missouri to be with her mom for a while and slowly Marly's eavesdropping on Chester's life turned into an addiction. At night, she listened for hours to his sad silence. Sometimes five or ten minutes would pass without even a squeak of sofa springs or a sigh or shuffle across the linoleum floor. And then she'd realize that she too had not heard the sound of her own movement either. He, as far as Marly could tell, stopped going to work and rarely left the apartment. She'd expected friends to stop by to cheer him up or for him to call someone to talk through his heartbreak, but there seemed to be no one for Chester to call.

For Walter, it was the detail about the Havahart traps more than anything that made him question his role in the dirty war. He'd never agreed with the rats plan, and at first, he thought it was because of his extreme dislike for Johnson, who had once grabbed Marly's ass while walking behind her up the stairs—"I just had to, baby. I mean it was, like, ripe." Afterward, Walter had punched him in the face. But truly, the rats—all things Johnson aside—was a cruel and childish act, and in the fever of vengeance, the entire complex relished in freeing snake-food into the unit while the unsuspecting victim, even after losing his girlfriend, chose to catch and release the rats instead of using poison. This kindness on Chester's part turned Walter's heart, and he no longer desired revenge; he suddenly and unequivocally liked Chester and this, the rats and collapse of his relationship, was all Marly and his fault.

Something clicked, and he couldn't bring himself to speak to anyone involved, not even Marly. After the rats, he began ignoring her phone calls and texts. He no longer went to her house and talked about the future, but instead, got up in the morning and walked the two miles to work and when the day was done, he walked home. But no matter how much he tried to exhaust himself, the guilt did not leave. Belinda and the other residents were in a triumphant state, drunk on power and conquest, but 2-C remained quiet and locked, only the dim light of table lamps seeping beneath the door let anyone know that Chester was home. Damn Chester, Walter thought, for kidnapping Gloria, whom Walter now imagined with a missing finger. He hated this duplicitous nature: violence and caring.

Marly knew Chester's performance was days away and that he now had to proceed without The Electric Companion. As far as she could tell, he had not tried to find a replacement, as if by leaving the position open Dorothy would return. But Dorothy did not, and the few times Marly heard Chester's voice over those lonely days listening in on his life, he spoke to Dorothy's answering machine, begging her to return, promising a better life that he could not provide. This, Gloria's apartment, was the best he could offer. Marly knew his suffering. Walter had taken her back, or so she thought, into his heart again, and just when she was getting comfortable, that fool began ignoring her like he had when they split up. She thought about going after Butter just to hurt Walter the way he was causing her pain by not returning her calls and texts. What kind of person did that, Marly often thought, just straight up stopped communication without a reason?

Once, she listened to Chester cry. The recording was from 3:00 a.m. the night before but she'd just gotten home from work and had opened a bottle of wine. She shared silence with Chester for nearly an hour, just the white noise picked up from electric currents and refrigerators and functioning AC units, all the imperceptible frequencies within a multi-unit building, and then, suddenly, he sobbed. It began as a hiccup but rose into a snotty wail and as soon as Marly heard the pitch shift into grief, she too began to sob, as if his sobbing triggered within her such deep sorrow that she experienced simultaneously her own hurt as well as the shock of this stranger's pain. They stayed this way for half an hour at least, both crying, sharing intimacy across time and space. And then, just as briskly as the crying had begun, it stopped, and Chester stood and walked out of the living room; in the background, she heard the sound of running water.

The Friday afternoon before Chester's performance, Marly settled into listening through his previous afternoon's routine. She rewound the recording she'd transferred early that morning before going to work and pressed play when she heard the rumblings of his movements. It was Thursday morning for Chester. He seemed in good spirits. After he made coffee and toast and paced back and forth, humming a tune Marly did not recognize, he dialed a number on his cell phone, the volume so loud Marly could hear the chime of each tapped digit.

"Tito," he said. "Chester. How is Grandma? She did what? That's crazy. I've never seen her outside of this apartment. It's hard to imagine her at the park. I know. Yeah, my pops would flip his shit if he knew his brother was looking after Gloria. It's just for a time—All right—Yeah—I'll come after the performance. I dunno. San Jose is, what, an hour? Like, three or four I think. You're right, Tito. I'll put up in a hotel and come in the morning."

Marly texted Walter immediately: "Gloria is in San Jose."

"See you tonight?" he texted back.

She wrote and deleted a number of irate texts that unfurled her rage and torment in logical bullet points but knew that would do no good, that he would mope and apologize or disappear entirely, and so she simply replied: "I'll wait out front of the theater."

Walter walked and fantasized about an installation project. He was drenched in sweat and all of his limbs felt heavy and loose, and this, he thought, this exhaustion mixed with elation and blood and sweat had so much internal sound that he began to hear music made from his body's movement. But this idea could not exist without visuals, he realized, there needed to be a sight experience that was disparate from, but correlative to the body in motion. He imagined a long line of spectators, all waiting to put on a single virtual reality headset. The footage, though he'd yet to discover what they might watch, would be very different than the sounds his body made. Perhaps bucolic or violent, he did not know. What excited him was the urgency he felt while thinking of what this footage could be and how the viewer might respond emotionally to the anachronistic sensory experience. He thought of Marly. He wanted somehow to include her in this performance piece, if not her person, then ways unique to how she saw the world, and then she texted—"Gloria is in San Jose"—and he laughed.

They met outside of the double brass and glass doors of the theater; Marly was dressed in a blue gown and Walter wore slacks and a blazer over a black button-up. He smiled when he saw her and leaned in for a hug, but she silently pushed him away. No words this time, just an expression of extreme sadness and defeat.

"I'm sorry, Marly."

"Don't," she said. "The show has already started."

A diminutive man past eighty led them down the aisle to their seats near the stage. It was a good turnout, Marly thought, for a magician. Walter, too, had not known what type of audience to expect, but this group seemed to be a mixture of older, well-off men and women dressed in fine clothes and a smattering of college students wearing sweaters and tights and jeans. Neither Marly nor Walter had done any research into what type of performer Chester was because they had been so caught up in dismantling his presence in 2-C. It was somewhat shocking when the announcer began his introduction of The Amazing Professor Chess.

"Tonight, you will experience a legendary event of supernatural proportions. Never before has science and magic been welded in such a way to convey violence and healing, terror and relief all at once. Beware! You will witness gory acts done to the body that no human should ever have to experience, but know that with his own glorious intellect Professor Chess has devised a potion that rejuvenates and heals the body no matter the infliction!"

Walter was enthralled, and he looked to Marly, nearly reaching for her hand but when he saw her pinched expression, he knew that his touch was not welcome. She nodded curtly and said, "We're in for it now."

"I'm sorry I ignored you," Walter tried again. "This time it was necessary and I had—"

"Shut up, and watch the show, Wal."

Chester had walked onto the stage. Marly saw that his make-up gave him a grave demeanor. In his tuxedo and shined Italian loafers, Chester looked regal almost, not small at all. Chester stood alone. He clasped his hands professorially behind his back, and with solemn speech, he announced that his "beautiful, electric companion" had vanished during last night's performance. He did not know, he said, whether she was carried into another plane through the electrical current or had evaporated as water heated in a pan. He was praying for her return, and he hoped, he told the audience, that they would pray too. An audible inhalation spread throughout the audience once Chester finished his speech, and all around them, people whispered and sighed until Professor Chess held up his hands for them to silence.

"Tonight, I will be accompanied by Mr. Larkin whom you all know as the kindly gentleman who led you to your seats. Please welcome my one-time assistant—"

With a sweep of the hands, he brought the old man to his side, and they stood this way, together, until the applause died down. "Mr. Larkin. Are you prepared to inflict violence onto my person? Do you promise not to hesitate when I tell you to cut and slash?"

"I do," Mr. Larkin said, sniggering as if waiting on a punch line he knew to anticipate.

"I have been so lonely for companionship," Professor Chess began: "For years, I have searched for a mate who knows the path I have walked, who will step in time with me through the ages and this endeavor has proven difficult. But tonight, ladies and gentlemen I tell you: I have found my match! And because I love you all so much, because you, my audience, are my family, I ask that you join me as witnesses to my marriage!"

The crowd exploded in applause so loud that Marly startled, rose in her seat and looked around at all of these beaming faces. She saw joy, but she also saw something similar to Mr. Larkin's expression, something knowing and malicious. Walter too found himself eyeing the people on the aisle across from him, feeling like a sad, stupid man on the outside of a joke.

"Mr. Larkin, if you would please lock this crate once I am inside?"

Chester stepped into a coffin that sat on top of a raised platform. It was small and his head and feet stuck out of both ends. He wiggled his toes and asked Mr. Larkin to bring the saw.

"Are you ready, Mr. Larkin? Remember do not hesitate."

Mr. Larkin nodded and began to saw through the wood and then through Chester's body, and Chester screamed in pain and blood dripped from the wooden box, so much blood that it pooled on the floor beneath, and Mr. Larkin, breathing with difficulty now, slipped when the blood seeped under his loafers. Then Chester was silent. The lights dimmed and he looked dead; he had to be dead if the blood was real. Marly heard a man snuffle behind her. Then, loud and obtrusive in this moment of shock and grief, the sound system blared "Here Comes the Bride." A preacher stepped from side stage and stood at an altar. A spotlight illuminated center stage, and Mr. Larkin grabbed ahold of one end of the casket and pulled Chester apart; he was now separated from his feet. Mr. Larkin dragged his torso to the right of the preacher, and his legs to the left and the ceremony began.

"Do you, Loyal Feet take Professor Chess as your lawfully wedded husband, to have and to hold, in sickness and in health?" The toes waggled and the two loafers clicked together happily. The audience erupted in laughter, and Chester winked and beamed with pride and love at his own feet. "Do you Professor Chess take as your lawfully wedded wife, to have and to hold—"

"Oh, get on it with! I do. I do. Come here, darlings," he said.

Mr. Larkin pushed his feet so that the toes faced Chester's mouth, and he kissed the shining loafers again and again until the stage went dark, and the audience clapped and whistled and the lights did not come back on until the room had quieted once more.

Chester returned whole. "Some of you may be skeptics, perhaps saying to your companion that I am a crook, a liar, that there was some contraption in the box that allowed me to be cut in half and then resurrected in my original form. Fair enough," he said. "I will prove to you that my rejuvenation potion works. Mr. Larkin. Please bring out the chopping block and hatchet. Mr. Larkin will chop off my finger right here in front of you, and without a box and in plain view, you will witness my finger regrow before your very eyes!"

Walter looked to Marly, and they moved closer to the stage, squinting into the bright lights. Chester put his hand on the chopping block and asked Mr. Larkin to ready the hatchet and he counted—"One. Two. Three."—and Mr. Larkin brought the blade down and blood spurted onto the front row and Chester screamed in agony, holding his bloodied hand, allowing more blood to flow down his white shirtsleeves and cover his tuxedo jacket. It looked so real that Marly's stomach heaved, and Walter looked away and on the butcher block there was a finger.

"Here, see for yourself," Chester called, and it felt to Walter as if he looked right at him when he threw the severed finger. Walter and Marly watched as it sailed, vanishing momentarily in the spotlight overhead and then landed a few feet in front of where they sat before it rolled carefully to the edge of the carpeted aisle and stopped.

Marly grabbed Walter's hand then, she squeezed and squeezed again, and he turned to her, nuzzled his face against her neck. "The finger," he said. "It's the finger."

—

ONE HOUR SOUTH of Oakland, in San Jose, Gloria Pendejada sat in the backyard of her daughter's ex-husband's brother's house coloring in an adult coloring book Chester had mailed to her a few days before. The sun had just dropped behind the rooftops and everything was cast in mauve and Gloria watched for a moment, waiting for the color to darken into night. She lit a cigarette and two of the four children that lived at Tito's accidentally rammed into her chair playing some infernal game that involved chasing and falling and screaming.

"Ay, niñas! Stop all this craziness. Don't you like to color?"

The two children, both girls nodded: each wearing pink dresses and pink bows who were different in age but looked as if they could be twins.

"You don't want your abuela out here coloring on her own, do you? Not when she can have such lovely girls to color with her?"

Delighted by the compliments and the new game, the two girls ran into the house followed by a cry of dismay from their mother who was cooking in the kitchen and a reprimand from Tito for running in the house. Gloria inhaled on her cigarette and laughed at the uproar she'd caused.

REMBRANDT BEHIND
WINDOWS

REMBRANDT BEHIND
WINDOWS

ALL DAMIEN WANTED to do was pilfer what was left of Moms.

The light had changed in her room. Not just the light but also the air. Like he'd stepped into a still life painting of his moms without his moms in frame, but still there, you know. Like how the first time he'd snuck in her room, he noticed a painting his folks had salvaged from a church that was hidden behind a stack of windows that stood almost to the ceiling. He knew the painting. A Rembrandt he'd studied in honors history: a naked lady on the bed, the sheets crumpled and twisted. There was this dude creeping behind a curtain wearing a baggy-ass hat, and maybe from the vantage point of a newcomer, he was still unseen, but she, Danaë, *she* was all in light. The light was Zeus. His folks didn't own shit like this, or even care about art, and the Rembrandt didn't add up to what he knew about Moms. So, he kept coming back, pussyfooting, as Pops called it, trying to learn more because he felt now that he'd never known a true thing.

Damien had always hated coming into his parents' bedroom before—hollering "good night" from the doorway as Moms lay in a purple nightgown, and Pops was spread-eagle in briefs like anybody wanted to see his hairy-ass self. Now he was in his parents' room every night, every day, just trying to catch a smell of her: saw-dust, lavender, and cheap-ass detergent. Not like his tired-ass pops who put on a good show, faking like he hadn't been sleeping on the recliner, shoving the comforter beneath the couch before Damien got up each morning, but in truth Pops hadn't slept in his own bed for, what, a month?

Damien closed the curtains, wiped dirt from the sheets. On top of Moms' dresser, crowded with dumb figurines—the poodle-shaped perfume dispenser, the dolphin swimming along ceramic waves, blue bottles with tiny mouths—were prescriptions, hand lotion, a Christie Mystery, and two packs of Capri Slims. All as before. He used to love watching Moms smoke, the way she blew out a thick white cloud and then sucked it up through her nose. French, she called it. Her voice, the smoke, it tore him up to remember, made his shoulders shake and snot drip from his nose, but he pilfered this too—the straight-bawling—from her room. *What the fuck ever,* he thought, stuffing both packs of Slims in his pocket, revived now that he'd stolen something.

Metal ringlets jingled when he pulled open each dresser drawer in turn. He was looking for surprises, like the Rembrandt, but hoping to find nothing save ordinary. The top two drawers, petite and inset, were full of cotton panties, but his hand ran across something silken and lacey with alligator clips, and he pulled it out all in one tangle. What the purple waistband was he didn't know, but the garter belt he recognized instantly. Durg's sister, Penny, wore a black one around her neck like a collar. Penny's neck was long and thin, and she always cut the collars from her T-shirts. He shoved the garter and lacey belt deep into his pocket and got the hell out.

Damien pedaled the two miles over to the purple house that killed his mother, racing hard against the fall wind, cold tears streaming down his face. He dropped his BMX at the backdoor and grabbed the key from beneath a frog-shaped planter, and he let himself inside.

When his moms got sick, they'd been in the process of tearing out the walls, opening the place up so this tiny-ass house might have more flow (so different than his crib where every square inch was taken up by random junk from his parents' construction company: old doors, tools, siding, and sinks). J and M Construction firm had folded under the weight of Moms's hospital bills, but Pops finished this particular house on his own, refusing to sell even though the market had spiked. Pops had painted every room a different shade of purple. Even the exterior was violet and lavender—the living room was mauve, the kitchen was a deep purple, and the bathroom where the black mold had been was Royal. One room in every house they finished had been painted Royal, her signature. "Know why it's called that?" When she'd asked him, he'd been in the fifth grade and interested in invertebrates, the ocean. "The color comes from the mucus of sea snails. Only royalty had purple robes, you know."

Damien closed himself in the bathroom. His lungs opened—*swoosh*, like dropping down the water slide at Adventure River—and a crying jag hit him unawares, but he sucked it back, snorting up the tears until he coughed. There was no black mold now. Men in biohazard suits had torn the rest of the bathroom away, ran tests on the entire house. That didn't help Damien none. The mold had been hidden, no sign of it at all in that once dandelion-wallpapered room where everything was stained tawny from nicotine. When Moms busted out the walls with a gorilla bar, she did not know the mold was there. Damien thought about her coma, the pneumonia steadily beating down all antibiotics. It was the same, wasn't it? No signs of dying showed on her face because all the sickness existed on the inside.

Standing in the tub next to a frosted window above the soap tray, Damien lit his first cigarette. The smoke went down harshly, and he hacked. He practiced French, like Moms, collecting the smoke in his cheeks and letting it sift slowly out, trying but failing to suck the white cloud up through his nostrils. She made it look so easy. He tried, again. The toothpick-sized cigarette held daintily between his lips. He did not feel tough but weirdly sexual, like he was kissing it, and suddenly, with the urgency of having forgotten something very important, he pulled out the garter and ran his fingers across the silky center, pinching it with his thumb. It was stretchy, and the lace did not feel coarse, not the way he'd always imagined Penny's garter itched her skin; no, it felt soft and inviting. *A dumbass thing*, he thought, about Penny, *to wear this around your neck*. He was fighting off an image of Moms acting sexy, of her standing nearly nude in a doorway. She'd once been young, like Penny. Before she'd had Damien, before she'd melded her desires with the house and work, she had wanted to be sexy for Pops. He'd never thought of Moms as anything but an overbearing hard-ass that controlled his Play Station time and only let him stay over at Durg's once a month. Moms had pushed him to get into seventh grade honors, then eighth, and now, he was in all AP courses, and he hated how little time he had for dicking off with Durg who was 100 percent gen. pop. And as he pulled his pants down and off, he did not try and stop the coming tears, but let the snot bubble, let strings of saliva hang from his lips, falling, straight-nasty, like some living thing, like some sea snail bleeding purple. He slid the garter onto his thigh. It fit snugly, the silk like cool water against his skin.

When he got home, Damien found Pops half-asleep on the recliner, *Married… with Children* blasting from the TV. Damien avoided his sad eyes and threw himself down on the couch heavy-like so his mood televised broader than Al Bundy. Damien was tired, too.

"What's up with dinner?"

Pops pulled a cigarette free with his teeth and lit it. Smoke curled under his Lennon eyeglasses, and he rubbed the ache away with a dirty fingernail. "See what's in the kitchen," he said. "Not hungry myself."

Pops was still wearing work clothes: ratty, old white tennis shoes, blue jeans covered in paint and joint compound, a flannel unbuttoned over a dark purple J and M Construction shirt—Jim and Molly. Moms, Molly, would've made dinner had she been there. Tired and dressed identically as this lazy-ass man, she would cook up some chicken or at least throw a pizza in the oven. *Her face.* Damn if he would cry in front of Pops. If he did, he knew what would come next: Pops kneeling, petting Damien like he was five years old. Nah, he told himself, just breathe through. But her face was there in his mind's eye, her blonde hair, thin and shiny; her pale skin like paper with microscopic freckles around her eyes; her eyes copper with little flakes of gold all broken up like light reflecting off shards of broken glass. Damien stuffed his hands into his pockets, a protective reflex he'd owned since he was old enough to wear pants. With his hands hidden, no one could see him clench his fists, digging his nails into his palms until the pain grew intolerable. He felt the lumpy lace of Moms's garter belt around his thigh, and this calmed him. He'd stolen one of her secrets, and now that everything seemed so damn transparent, he longed for secrecy, for some private knowledge, only they shared.

Pops snored in the recliner beside him, a Pall Mall burning down between his calloused fingers. *Secrets, right?* Damien reached into his bag and pulled out the stolen pack of Slims. Slowly, he brought a cigarette to his lips. Pops's snore deepened when Damien grabbed the Zippo and—*chink-chink*—sparked the flint. He let the flame hang close, but did not light up.

Damien stashed the Slims into his backpack and went to the kitchen to see about dinner. In the fridge, he found molded cheese and a sweating plastic bag with bologna inside. Durg had food. His fridge was always stocked. Penny might have some weed.

Damien's best friend, Freddy Durango, was the only fifteen-year-old he knew that still wanted to play Magic the Gathering during sleepovers, and when Damien came barreling through the basement door, unannounced and hollering like he was being chased by something, Durg jumped, Nintendo controller ripping from the console, and bolted the door closed all like *WTF.*

"I'm just fucking with you."

"Why you even here?"

"I'm hungry and your mom probably ordered in from somewhere. Am I right? What, like, pizza? Hoagies? Nah. It's Chinese."

Durg nodded, told Damien there was Chow Mein from Royal Dragon.

When Damien came back down to the basement, carrying a to-go container of cold Chinese food, he asked after Penny. Durg didn't pause the game or look up. "Where you think?"

Damien wanted to run to Penny's door, ask after some weed or a DVD, acting like he could give a fuck if she wanted to share or not, if she wanted to be near him or not. Damien had to finesse his love for Penny so Durg never got jealous. So, he shrugged his shoulders all, like, *who cares,* and he ate the clumped, slimy noodles from Royal Dragon. He even sat for ten minutes or more after he finished just to prove to Durg he wanted nothing to do with his sister.

"I gotta piss," Damien said and skipped from the basement, up the stairs, and into the little hall where Penny's door stood across from the bathroom. He knocked, listened. Her The Cure poster hung on her door, above the knob, and his ear almost touched Robert Smith's mouth. He heard the rustling of Penny's comforter and her soft padding across the room. "What?" her voice, dull and irritable, came from inside.

"It's Damien. You hooked up?"

She opened the door. Her head barely reached Damien's chin, and he liked that she made him feel tall even though he was short. Her tiny fingers tugged at the lace band around her neck. Damien thumbed his own garter through the pocket of his jeans.

"I'm busy," she said. Damien saw a pile of eyeballs and mouths cut from various magazines strewn across her bed.

"With what?" he asked.

"Don't be a bitch, Pen," Durg called from the basement.

Penny rolled her eyes. "Give me a minute."

When she came out of her room, Penny demanded Durg stop playing Nintendo so she could watch *Pulp Fiction.*

"That movie is so damn stale, Pen."

"My weed, my pick. Besides, you know you like Uma, Freddy. I see the way your hand disappears in your pockets when you watch *Kill Bill.* Next to your sister? That's sick."

Durg let out a long, bratty-ass sigh before he shut down the system. He threw himself between Damien and Penny. Penny pulled a joint from behind her ear.

"We got to wait," she said.

"For what?"

"For the 'royale with cheese.'"

When Penny finally lit the joint, Samuel L. Jackson was quoting from the bible. But Damien had long since lost focus, the word Royal playing him like a yo-yo, bringing back memory upon memory like sneezing fits, and he feared their disappearance, feared that each flash, bright—horribly fucking bright—would be lost. There weren't enough memories, he thought. He was too young. *What then*? he asked himself a second time. *When I'm old and stupid and tired and sitting in front of* Married... with Children— *what will I remember of Moms?* There was so much to remember and yet he was just a kid, he knew that, and he knew soon he'd be like Pops, like Moms was before she died—tired and distracted, not young anymore.

He took Penny's joint between his fingers, inhaled deep and did not cough. He was proud of this. Soon, he was mired in a heavy high, and *Pulp Fiction* ended, and Durg was saying he wanted to go to bed, offering to set up a blow-up mattress for Damien. But Damien said, no. Said he needed to get back home.

"Smoke one more with me." Penny was smiling at him with this shy glance full of meaning and expectation that straight freaked Damien out because that's the way he'd always wanted her to look at him since he was, like, nine years old. "Yeah, all right," he said.

Durg scoffed, sulked off to his bedroom, and slammed the door. Ever since Freddy and Damien had met in third grade, Durg had feared Damien would like Penny more. Only recently had Durg's suspicions drifted toward sex. Before, he just didn't want Damien to start liking The Misfits and Shakespeare.

When Damien brought his attention back to Penny, her face was so close that he saw wet in her eyes; her lips parted, showing bright, sharp teeth. "What's it like?" she asked. "Our family is fucked up, but I can't imagine—"

She passed Damien the joint, the rotting smell of cannabis wafted inches from his nose. He couldn't bring himself to hit the weed, not yet, not if he was hearing Penny right. He felt everything, that's how, and nothing.

"I'm sorry," Penny said. "Stupid to ask."

Damien shook his head. It wasn't stupid to ask. And he wanted to tell her about the Rembrandt behind windows in his parents' room, about the woman laid up in bed with her hand raised toward Zeus, presumably alone, but not alone. The painting was about secrets, about the lighted places and the shadows where little peeping-ass squires wait to blow the whole thing up. He looked at Penny, trying to form words, and she kissed him. Her breath tasted like ash and the cola she'd been drinking. He kissed her back, hard, like they'd kissed before, but he hadn't ever, like, with anybody. Damien felt shaky and shit because he wanted her so bad and had for so long, and yet she'd kissed him only after asking about Moms and that made him angry, and in some fucked switcheroo, it made him want her more. Penny straddled his lap, made *hmmm* noises when he touched her breasts. He pulled at the waistband of her shorts, tugging down from behind so that he could feel the sheen of her panties.

She grabbed his hands. "No.No.No," she said, through scrunched together lips.

Damien didn't listen and kept pulling. He was intent on feeling the hidden places where no one but Penny's hand moved. She jerked her face away.

"Rule number one, asshole, and it's better you learn from me," she said. "Never keep going after a girl says 'no.'" Her disappointment, her hurt, her taut jaw.

He shook his head. "Just forget it." He tried to wiggle from beneath her weight.

"God!" Penny punched him in the chest, but he didn't feel pain.

Damien eased into the dark kitchen, shutting the back door with a faint *click*.

"Don't pussyfoot on my account." He heard Pops's voice a second before a thick, hard hand clutched the meat of his upper arm and sent him crashing into the fridge.

"Where the fuck you been? Too big to tell me when you go out?" Pops flipped on the light. Two large pizza boxes sat closed on the table. "Didn't order this shit to go to waste."

Damien could smell pepperoni and cheese, and he wanted some. He wanted to sit in front of the TV and eat slice after slice until he was bloated and sick, while Pops curled up in his makeshift bed on the recliner. He wanted to lean back and smoke, talk about how shitty the Braves were playing that season—*Pass me the ashtray, son.* But Damien could not stop thinking about Penny, the smooth skin of her thigh. The smell of vanilla oil was all over him, and he wanted so badly to be beneath her weight on the Durangos' couch.

"I ate," Damien mumbled. Pops had never hit him before, never raised his voice.

"What?" he asked. "Speak up, man."

"I'm not hungry, okay."

"Oh, that's funny. Last I heard, you wanted dinner."

The next morning, Damien walked inside Walgreens like he was eighteen, not fifteen and skipping school. He scanned the pharmacy aisle for Robitussin. All night he had dreamed of Penny, her eyes squinting with confusion and hurt, and pizza and his father shoving him against the fridge. He dreamt of Moms. He wanted to make things right with Pops, but they were so different. What was he supposed to say? He didn't feel sorry, not really, no, he was straight-pissed. He wanted Pops to sleep in his room again and for Moms to drive him to school in the morning, shoving a gross-ass pack of Lunchables into his hands like he was still nine years old. But with Penny, he hoped, like, if he could just make her laugh, then she'd forgive him. He could do that, right?

"Shouldn't you be in school?" A woman around Moms's age stood at the cash register, pretty in her own right, with thick cleavage pushing out the top of a low-cut dress. *I got bird bones* Moms used to tell Damien. In his memory, she wore a purple tank top, low cut, and her ribs spread out from her sternum like the imprint of fingers drug across sand. *Bird bones can't hold curves like some women, or they'd break.*

"For my mother," Damien told the cashier. "She's sick."

Damien rode over to the purple house, the rhythmic tick-tacking of bearings in the hub of his back rim as he coasted along narrow residential streets. He didn't care if anyone stole his bike when he tossed it aside in the drive, didn't care that he wanted a cigarette. Not anymore. He knew he was the creep behind the drapes, that silly-ass jester watching Zeus's coming light. What else could a fifteen-year-old boy do but peep grown-up shit from shadows?

Damien thought about how he'd helped Moms the day the realtor dropped off keys to the purple house. Pops was at the bank. She'd pounded plaster from the kitchen walls with her gorilla bar as Damien followed behind, popping lath off rough-hewn studs with a crowbar. Her mouth and nose were hidden behind a thin paisley bandana while a double-filtered oxygen mask had dwarfed Damien's head. *Why was I even there?* And if he hadn't been there, he knew now, she would have worn the respirator instead. In the bathroom now, he imagined knocking down walls. *Swoosh. Smash.*

He imagined plaster raining in giant clumps, rifts torn in dandelion wallpaper like flags among soot and dust. This is how the mold had entered her lungs.

He lit a Slim and blew French.

"Damien?" Pops called. "You here?"

He hadn't heard the door. He flushed the Slim. "Using the bathroom," he said.

"Don't clog the toilet. Prospectives always ask about plumbing."

Prospectives? Prospectives meant couples with newborns, couples with no kids, or couples with five kids. Prospectives meant rich college students whose parents tagged along quietly in the background, making mental notes of all things wrong with the place.

Damien unlatched the lock. "Since when?"

"Just came back from the realtor's office. It's time."

Pops sat on the floor across from Damien; his head leaned against the wall. His beard thick with gray. The way Pops looked now, eyes fixed upward, reminded Damien of when Moms was in the hospital. She had tubes in her nose and mouth and her arms. She wore a thin paper gown. Pops had asked the nurse to dress her in something comfortable, but the nurse told him *no*. He had pushed past her and into a supply closet and dug through drawers, looking for scrubs. It had taken two security guards to cuff Pops to a chair, and he'd banged his head against the wall, yelling, *Get her out of that paper, goddamn it. Dress her comfortably*. What if Pops never came back, Damien thought, never again slept in his old room? What if this man was his father now?

His pops leaned forward, gripping Damien's knee. "We'll get through this. We will."

Damien could see Penny reading in bed when he knocked on her window. She popped up, grabbing a baseball bat from behind her nightstand.

"It's Damien."

"The fuck, Damien? Come to the door like a normal person."

He pressed the bottle of Robo to the window and said, "Let's trip, Pen."

She was waiting for him in the basement. Durg was immersed in some upper level Sonic the Hedgehog that Damien had never before seen. Freddy loved the old systems: Nintendo, Sega. Hell, the fool even played Atari.

"Don't you have other friends?" Penny asked.

"If we ever make out," Damien said. "I promise I will not touch you."

Durg threw down his controller mid-game and stood like he was about to swing on Damien, but he didn't step, "What the fuck you just say to my sister?"

"It's cool, Freddy," Penny said. "It won't ever happen again."

Freddy was all red faced, and Penny was still looking like *come on motherfucker. Tell me why I should be nice?* Damien tossed Robos to each of the siblings. He threw himself on a round papasan. He hated this fucking chair because the dog slept there, and once, back when they were in fourth grade, Damien had found a turd.

"What the hell is this?" Durg asked.

Damien didn't answer. He popped the childproof seal and downed the bottle in one extended gulp. The stuff tasted acrid, sweet. "Cheers."

They watched him, anger slipping away until he saw a little shimmer of *oh it's on now!* Penny bit into the plastic seal, pulled it away with her teeth. Damien watched Freddy. The less he saw Penny do anything with her mouth the happier he'd be, like, forever. Durg downed his bottle and snatched up his controller, dragging out his anger. "Don't fuck with my sister."

"You're not my daddy. If I want to fuck Damien, you don't have a say."

"I'm not talking to you, Pen. I'm telling Damien how it is."

All Damien heard was *fuck*. He told himself Penny didn't mean it that way. She'd accidentally dropped a couple prepositions—*to* fuck *with*—by accident. Damien curled into the shit-stained papasan, slipping his hands into his pockets. He was still wearing the garter.

When the Robo kicked in, all color and sound ballooned, and Damien could not hold onto any true thing—Moms planting seeds in the garden. She wore a sun hat. She wore brown shorts. A wheelbarrow. Manure. On her wrist, a watch glinted—her gorilla bar burst through plaster and stayed—Moms driving with the radio playing oldies, laughing and tickling Damien. *Car dance, Damien!* She wiggled her arms back and forth, and he giggled as the singer crooned in high falsetto about the jungle. He couldn't hold on, like, choking. He coughed, a captured spike. It was too much, the rolling dreams. Damien covered himself with an afghan pulled from the back of the papasan and watched the room through holes in the cross-stitch. He curled deeper into the blanket. Purple dots popped in the darkness, and if he squeezed his eyes shut, bigger explosions pulsed. The purple air grew humid, and he giggled and the giggling spread through his body and turned to strong and unstoppable laughter. Sweat slipped from his chin. He saw light. When he slipped headfirst from the folds of the afghan, and his head crowned, he saw his mother's face over her belly, bloodshot and wet with tears. The air caught on his skin. He screeched. And he fell to the floor with a hard, weighted *thunk*. The room blurred, then brightened, until it nearly broke apart with light, and there was Penny and Durg, arms touching as they watched Sonic stand motionless, shrouded in a sparkling sphere.

"Let's get out of here," Damien said and left the basement before either sibling had a chance to stand. He snatched up his BMX from where he'd left it just outside of Penny's window and walked toward the tracks.

"Wait, Damien," the siblings called at the same time.

Mica shimmered up at Damien from the black asphalt. Houses with two, sometimes three levels stood on elevated yards. The night was cool, and Penny was without a jacket. She rubbed her arms. Durg rapped under his breath, repeating the same harmony again and again, mouthing vowels, sounds without meaning.

They reached a set of railroad tracks—a distant car alarm. A crack of white light unzipped the dark. He lit a Slim and watched smoke drift upward. Moms's satin garter felt chilly and tight against his skin. The ground vibrated with the weight of an oncoming train. When the engine came into view, everything succumbed to the sound of passing freighters. Damien stepped closer, feeling the wind as it moved through his hair and pushed through his sinuses and pressed against his closed eyes. He waited, trying to determine the break between cars by listening to the change in rhythm—a solid *WOOSH* before a hollow *WISH. WOOSH-WISH.* A hand grabbed through the darkness and held onto his arm. He opened his eyes briefly and saw Penny. Durg was slouching, arms crossed over his chest but he too had shut his eyes. The engine, beyond them now, blew a whistle that cut through the racket of steel wheels on track. Penny squeezed, her fingers cold. Fainter still, the train whistle blew. And in his mind's eye, Damien saw his pops and moms sitting together on the white sofa with colored flowers, saw how Pops nuzzled his nose into her hair, how she smiled and kissed the side of his lips.

Damien mounted his BMX in motion, and as he pedaled away, he heard Penny and Durg yell after him. The wind bit his cheeks, but the cold felt new.

He locked his bike up at his house and went inside, breathless but awake. The TV was on. Pops was asleep, snoring in the recliner with the comforter draped across his body, a pillow spilling over the chair arm. Damien went to his own room, grabbed a blanket and pillow, and tossed them on the sofa. He stripped to his boxers and rolled down Moms's garter from his thigh. He lay on his back in the shifting glow of silent sitcoms, and he thought about

Penny and the smooth skin of her palm. And he saw again how Moms once smiled, how Pops rested his head against her neck, and he tugged a Slim free, lit it with the zippo he'd pilfered.

"What the hell are you doing?" Pops had leaned forward, watching Damien from deep-sleep.

"Going to bed," he said.

His pops tilted back toward dreams. "Night, Damien."

HEADS DOWN

HEADS DOWN

DARREL COULDN'T REMEMBER whether tails up or tails down made a penny lucky. Whichever way, heads down is how he found the penny in the neglected commercial lot where he liked to go and think. Back when Darrel was a boy, his daddy worked as a car salesman in one of these lots—no cars now, just crabgrass and some other weeds Darrel didn't know the name of that grew tall and spindly with leaves and branches like trees.

Darrel left the penny and walked over to his truck, grabbed a beer, and twisted the cap off in the crook of his elbow. His daddy's briefcase sat on the bench next to the cooler. Darrel had waited thirty-four years to know what his daddy kept in that briefcase only to find a .357 Colt, a blank spiral notebook, and a pen with a lady in a bikini on it. In the shade of the truck cab, Darrel clicked the pen open and the lady's top vanished. Darrel thought about his wife, Pam, having to help be a pallbearer at his daddy's funeral—before she left him for the Coca-Cola driver who delivered to her waitress job. His uncle didn't like a woman carrying his brother, and Pam didn't like that she might chip the paint off her nails, but his daddy had no friends, hardly any family, and the funeral home was understaffed. Darrel's mama walked at the front of the procession and guided them through the cemetery, so no one stepped on any of the graves—"It'd be a damn shame if you bring bad luck on your daddy now that he's about to meet judgment with Jesus Christ," she'd said.

Darrel clicked the pen closed and the lady's bikini reappeared. He flipped the notebook open. Roger had told him, "If you have to take notes, make it so only you can understand." He'd written a word or two and numbered them based on what Roger deemed important. Next to *Colt* was the number one. Darrel pulled his daddy's .357 from the lid pocket of the briefcase. Opened the chamber, spun it—six bullets. A memory cropped up, of himself, about ten years old, shooting Coke cans with his daddy alongside the Mississippi River. He'd fired all six bullets and never nicked the red-and-white can. His daddy told him he couldn't shoot for shit and left Darrel there holding the warm gun. Long after the sun had set, his daddy came back and fetched him.

He'd written *Ten Grand* next to the number two. Darrel put the .357 under the seat and walked back over to the penny. Pam always bitched about his lack of drive to make money. Ever since he got laid off from the Little Debbie factory five years before, he'd been getting by on temp work or day labor. He cleaned pools, hung insulation, laid block, took down asbestos— that one paid damn good. After he couldn't afford the mortgage on his home, he moved Pam into his childhood bedroom at his mama's place. Darrel didn't mind the simple life, but Pam said she couldn't stand the boredom. If it weren't for Pam, he wouldn't need to think about luck. He'd have been sitting on the porch with some cold beer. He bent down at the knees and grabbed the penny. After wiping it on his pant leg, he pulled off his boot, and dropped the coin inside. "Make your own luck," Darrel said to the place where the penny had been.

Darrel climbed up in his truck and turned the ignition over. The clock on the dash read 2:45 p.m. He downed the rest of his beer and checked the list. *Mask* was written next to number three. With a flathead screwdriver, he unlocked the glove box and pulled out a black cotton ski mask. He took off his Atlanta Braves hat, dusted the bill with his fingers, and placed it inside the briefcase.

At Roxy's, Darrel parked around back like Roger had told him. A sign written in marker and taped to the basement door read: IF LOCKED GET KEYS FROM HELEN. Darrel put the ski mask in his back pocket, took the .357 from beneath the seat, and stuffed it in the front of his pants.

The bell rang when Darrel opened the door. Everyone turned around and watched him enter. Pam slouched back in the booth with pursed lips, her tiny frame nearly eclipsed by the Coca-Cola driver's wide shoulders. *Out of all the goddamn diners and Pam chose Roxy's,* Darrel thought. *Today.* She'd been angry with Darrel for so long he couldn't remember what her face was like when she smiled. Just beyond the counter was the door that led to the basement. The door had a little window that directly faced Pam. *Pam can't be no witness.* If temp work counted as dishonest, then robbing Roxy's would be downright sinful. The night Pam left, she told him not to expect her back. She said she'd found a man with an honest future. Darrel turned away from Pam and the deliveryman.

He found Roger in the back of the dining room. Darrel sat down in the booth, and Roger began to talk. Darrel couldn't concentrate. He knew what Roger had to say. The district and store manager will come at 3:30 with the payout from the other diners. Roger will follow them down to the basement. After he gets the money, he'll whistle "Dixie," and Darrel will go out through the front and meet Roger at the truck. Wear a ski mask; don't use real names. Roger had worked as a manager at Roxy's for fifteen years, but they fired him a few months back for stealing burger patties. Roger had filled his freezer full and sold them off to friends and neighbors. Darrel had even bought a few pounds. Since then, Roger had held up a taco truck and scored 200 bucks. Once, he flew to Texas and had his brother steal his luggage and then collected insurance money from the airline. After a while, Roger started wearing these pointy dress shoes and polyester slacks. He grew a mustache and took to saying things like "forget about it." In the booth, Darrel grabbed Roger's straw, chewed one end down to a point and then shoved that end into the other, making a square.

"You listening to me?"

"My wife's back there, Roger." Darrel pointed behind him, toward the door. He imagined Pam tapping her painted fingernails against her teeth and rolling her eyes back and keeping them all white the way she did.

The waitress came over, and Darrel ordered a beer.

"What you gonna do if the managers recognize you?"

"That's what the masks are for dipshit," Roger said. "Don't you ever think?"

Darrel turned around in his chair and leaned out into the aisle until he could see Pam's booth. The deliveryman blocked any view of her. She made him so damn nervous. Though he knew Roger had experience, the doubt he carried about robbing Roxy's grew stronger. Roger reasoned they had no other choice but to do the heist in the middle of the day, because neither of them knew how to break a safe.

Roger tapped the Formica table hard with his finger. "Pam? Forget about it. I don't give a damn if George W. is back there on a fucking Segway," Roger said. "This is important. Now listen, you ain't gonna drink that beer. I run a sober ship."

The waitress returned with Darrel's beer. Before Roger could stop him, he drank the whole thing in one long drink and set it off to the side.

"You stubborn ass—" Roger began, but the bell rang, and the managers walked in before Roger could scold him. Roger stood up.

The two managers walked up to the bar counter and talked to the waitress. One manager was fat with floppy jowls, and the other was so skinny he couldn't have weighed more than a buck o' five. Darrel slid out of the booth and followed Roger.

"You're walking funny," Roger said.

He pointed to his crotch. "My gun is rubbing up against me."

"Don't say gun, Darrel."

They passed the edge of the counter like they meant to go to the men's room. Pam looked out into the parking lot, and Darrel wondered what she found so interesting. After Roger slipped behind the basement door, Darrel followed. Once hidden, Roger pulled a purple ski mask over his face. Darrel pulled out his gun, checked the safety, and put it back in his pants a little closer to the hip this time. Roger gave a nod and clomped down the wooden steps.

"Get the fuck down!" Roger yelled.

Through the little window, Darrel had a clear view of his wife and the deliveryman. Pam smiled as they chatted. Darrel couldn't remember if he and Pam ever chatted. He could remember her smiling at him, but it'd been so long he'd forgotten how crooked her top teeth were. She rubbed her skinny thumb against the deliveryman's knuckles. Darrel thought they made a nice couple. There was no real way of knowing if he and Pam ever looked like a nice couple. He always thought of her as pretty, and he liked how he looked in his Atlanta Braves hat and Red Wing boots, but there was something different seeming about the way she acted with the deliveryman. He breathed deep. *Trust Roger. Look Out.* Darrel watched Pam get up and go outside. His confidence grew knowing she'd be gone. After the driver and Pam kissed and hugged by his big Coca-Cola truck, his wife got in her Oldsmobile and the man waved bye to her with only his fingers.

Roger had been down there a long time and had not yet whistled "Dixie." Darrel soft-stepped a few stairs and crouched where the wall ended and the steps opened out into the basement. The penny slid down and caught on his big toe. From his hiding spot, Darrel could see Roger had the man with jowls on the ground belly-down and Buck o' Five lay knocked out with blood around his head. Darrel watched Roger search through the open money-bag. Darrel regretted the penny. As a boy, his mama kept a swift hand ready for slip-ups, especially ones that would lead to bad luck. And the day after his daddy's funeral, his mama broke every mirror she could find. She put hats on the bed. Opened umbrellas in the house and left them. One day a robin flew in through the back door, a sure omen of death, and she trapped the bird inside. When Darrel and Pam came home later that evening, his mama had made ham and pie, while the bird banged into every closed window. But she kept living, and that made her crazy. Darrel leaned back against the stairwell and slid the penny-boot off his foot and thought *fuckfuckfuckfuck*. Roger heard the stair creak and caught sight of Darrel.

"Darrel, keep an eye on Phil."

Darrel stopped, flattened himself against the wall, felt chilly under his clothes. He slid his boot back on, but forgot to take out the penny. He pulled the ski mask from his back pocket and slid it on.

"Don't use my name, Roger. Damn it. You said not to use our real names."

"Darrel, put a gun on Phil." Roger pointed to the man with jowls.

Darrel crept the rest of the way down but didn't draw his gun. He grabbed the duffel bag, opened it, found videocassettes and envelopes full of receipts and bank slips.

"Where's the money, Roger?"

"What's the combination to the safe, Phil?"

"Why'd you hit the other guy?" Darrel said. "He's bleeding."

"Phil!" Roger squeaked.

Darrel pulled out his gun but didn't point it at anyone. "Damn it, Roger, where's the money?"

"We mo-mo-modernized. Nothing's in the safe."

"Then what's the fucking combination, Phil?!"

"3.32.21.4," Phil said. "Ain't no money in there. It goes straight to the bank now."

Roger flipped through the combination, opened the safe, revealing a 32-inch color television set playing an image of a public bathroom stall. Roger stood up and stepped back. A toilet. That's what Darrel saw. They looked on in silence for a moment. The waitress who brought Darrel the beer came on screen, opened the stall door, hiked her skirt up, and squatted. She sort of hovered over the toilet rather than sitting all the way down. Turning his head away, Darrel caught sight of beer boxes stacked in a far corner of the basement.

"What the fuck, Phil?" Roger said. He pointed the gun at the TV.

Phil stammered, "We got a website—"

The outside door opened, and the deliveryman dragged a dolly loaded with Coke bottles backwards into the basement. Roger spun around with the gun outstretched and fired. Darrel thought about how certain noises sound like a gun—fireworks, backfiring cars—but Darrel didn't think this gunshot sounded like those things. Inside the basement, the gunshot was like water-logged wood breaking against something solid: *dumph*. The lower half of the deliveryman's gray uniform turned liquid black. His movements reminded Darrel of spankings he got as a boy.

At home, the same night Darrel had failed to shoot the Coke can, his daddy took after Darrel with the belt. Darrel lurched forward with the blow, but his daddy jerked him right back. Darrel's mama sat on the divan and crocheted. "Think about your daddy's lashes, and it'll keep you from missing," she'd said.

The deliveryman cuddled himself on the ground and whispered, "God."

Roger swung the gun around: checked Phil who cried, checked Buck o' Five who made an *eewing* sound, checked the deliveryman who bled. Darrel imagined Pam waiting at home for the deliveryman the way that he wished she would wait for him. He couldn't remember a time she'd been sweet to him the way he saw her act in the diner booth. Darrel went to him. The sight of his blood brought bile to Darrel's mouth, but he choked it back.

"Help me, Roger," Darrel said.

"Help with what, Darrel?"

"Take him to the hospital."

Roger pointed his gun at Darrel. "Leave him, and we'll call an ambulance."

"He'll die before they come, Roger."

Darrel couldn't leave the man there to bleed to death. He didn't want him fucking his wife, but he didn't want anybody to die either.

Roger gritted his teeth and raised the gun more purposefully toward Darrel. "Give me your keys," Roger said.

"Why my keys?"

"I took the bus!" Roger stammered with the gun still held out. "YOU'RE MY GET-AWAY DRIVER!"

Darrel threw his truck keys at Roger, and they hit him in the chest. On his way out, he kept the gun trained on Darrel, stepping over the deliveryman and sliding between the dolly and door frame. Roger did not look at the man he'd shot or the stack of Cokes. Darrel heard the sound of the ignition hiccup, start, and then Roger burned rubber.

Phil hovered over Buck o' Five and whispered. Darrel didn't ask them for help. He fumbled in the deliveryman's pockets and found the keys to the Coca-Cola truck. Darrel lifted him up from under the shoulders, and the man's head draped back. His eyes lolled and sought focus. "Thank you," he said with a flimsy smile. "Masked avenger."

Out in the parking lot, Darrel dragged the man to the passenger side of the delivery truck. His blood felt warm down Darrel's pants and shirtfront. When Darrel's daddy was in the hospital, the last few days of his life, he had needed a bedpan and once, while emptying it, Darrel knocked it against the sink and the piss spilled all over his shirtfront and pants. Pam told him she'd grown tired of forgiving his clumsy ways.

"If I die, tell my girlfriend I've been happy these past weeks," the man said, as Darrel hefted him up onto the passenger seat of his truck. Darrel nodded and closed the door. *Happy. Shit.*

Happy? Darrel felt giddy like he imagined men who played and won at sports felt after a good game.

He walked back inside and told the two managers. "I'm the hero. I heard the shot and chased that guy off, right?"

Phil nodded. Buck looked to the TV as an elderly woman struggled with the buttons on her Capri pants.

At the hospital, Darrel ran inside the ER and yelled, "Man down." While nurses hauled the deliveryman out of the truck and onto a stretcher, he stood back. He didn't realize he was still wearing the ski mask until a pretty nurse in a baby blue uniform gave him a funny look. He took the mask off and nodded in apology.

"You did good bringing that man here," she said. "All our paramedics are called out to a burning donut shop downtown."

"That's my wife's boyfriend," he said.

Just past the emergency entrance, Darrel leaned against a lamppost, took off his boot, and shook the penny into his palm. He looked it over: 1981 minting. Darrel thought about flipping it off into the weeds, but instead, he put the penny back in his boot. From there, he walked. He wanted to watch the sunset but didn't know where one did such a thing, and so he kept on west, thinking eventually, the colors would shift and he'd see. He thought about Pam and all her meanness. He thought about his mama's house, and everything back home now seemed like nothing but mold and cold dampness. His mama and Pam never opened the curtains. They liked it dark inside and kept the windows barricaded behind thick drapes and some doily things. When he went home, he thought, he'd take those damn things down and never have a curtain cover a window again.

STRIKE ZONE

STRIKE ZONE

EVERYTHING FAMILIAR TO Gilbert had vanished into boxes labeled DINING ROOM or PANTRY. Papa's mineral collection no longer filled the display shelves. Plastic covered the living room couch and chairs.

He remembered how Mother used to pack the dishware and such before pest-control arrived, and so Gilbert removed his memory-journal from his pocket, or "Rerun" as his sister Mary-Beth called it, to see if an insect bombing was scheduled. He found nothing but recent food-logs and an afternoon visit to the zoo with Mary-Beth. How odd. He read that she had spent the day lip-locked with someone named Twyla while he had documented patterns within the insults of one particular orangutan: "It is not merely annoyance that causes this primate to brandish his middle finger, because some, like myself, who have done no offense are flipped the bird in the same manner as the boy who threw a soda can. Stranger still, others receive waves and clapping with no apparent provocation." Gilbert had no memory of that day, or any other day after 1985, but he understood the intrigue on part of his written-self.

He stood in the doorway and watched his sister, dressed in an ash-gray business suit and heels, fry bacon and eggs in the kitchen.

"If not for the apparent liquidation of all household accouterments, I would find it odd that you are not dressed in requisite muumuu and fuzzy slippers."

"A muumuu, Gil?" Mary-Beth asked. "I've been sober—" She cut it short, grinned. She felt too good today to let Gilbert get under her skin. Besides, Mary-Beth had no way of knowing what repetitions of daily life were actually engrained in Gilbert's mind and what he simply recovered from earlier journals. Truthfully, she *had* spent a good amount of time after his surgery drunk, wearing her housedress while she worked doing phone sex. Her customers of so many years—no longer, thank God—never saw her, and when they asked, Mary-Beth easily dressed her persona in whatever finery she wished.

"You don't like my fancy-people clothes?"

She studied Gilbert's downturned eyes and knew that he'd clicked out of cycle, the temporal hiccup—she loved that word, temporal, it's what the neurologist always said—usually took about thirty seconds before Gilbert returned. Behind his head, there was a clean square of paint where a photo of Papa smoking a cigar in front of his bookshelf had been until yesterday.

"Meeting the realtor," she said. "So we can get paid for the house."

Gilbert did not move from the doorway, but mumbled: "Trash, noun, 1518, worthless stuff, rubbish," he said. "Destroy or vandalize, 1970. Criticize severely, 1975—"

"We've gone over this," Mary-Beth said. "Twyla and I are moving into a house in that new subdivision by the Walmart."

"In this new subdivision by Walmart for which you do not need the definite article because it is only Walmart, of which there are many, and so the one we will be frequenting—"

"Enough," she said, and put down the spatula. "Come have breakfast, Gil."

Gilbert sat down at the table. Mother's vase was empty, sunlight flashing through the blown glass. She'd bought fresh flowers from the farmers' market on Sundays—before the car crash. He remembered the wreck vividly, not the event for which he was not present, but the jolt and exhaustion that came immediately after Mr. Weathers' assistant told him of the accident.

"When you go out this afternoon, pick up lilies for Mother's vase."

Mary-Beth eyed him from the stove. His neck hair needed trimmed. "Check your Rerun," she said. "Find the pink Post-it marked READ ME."

Gilbert traced the tablecloth's labyrinthine rose vines from left to right, as he had since childhood. When he reached the seam that interrupted the pattern, he stopped.

His mother stands at the stove and stirs potatoes with a wooden spoon. She whistles as she makes breakfast—"I'm So Tired" by The Beatles.

"I believe the intonation is higher, Mother." Gilbert sings, "Get myself a drink—" and raises his hand incrementally along with the lyrics as if stacking blocks. "Right, Papa?"

Papa reads The Daily *as he leans against the counter. A cup of coffee steams next to him.*

"Believe he's right, dear."

His mother stops whistling. Bacon grease spits against the wall.

"What's the capital of Latvia?" Papa asks.

Mary-Beth, sitting across the table from Gilbert, picks up petals that have fallen from the tiger lilies in the vase. She wears dark sunglasses and a black denim jacket.

"Riga," Gilbert answers. "That's easy."

"Sea turtle. Latin," his mother joins in. Gilbert loves when they both play trivia.

"Green, leatherback, or loggerhead?"

"Loggerhead."

"Caretta caretta," he says. "My favorite."

"I know, Doodle," she says.

Mary-Beth takes off her sunglasses. "You guys disgust me."
"Be nice," Mother says.

She kisses Mary-Beth on the forehead. Mary-Beth shrinks away from Mother's affection. Gilbert gathers the long yellow petals Mary-Beth has scattered and stacks them in three piles, three high. There are two extras, and with these, he covers the lenses of Mary-Beth's sunglasses.

"Breakfast is served, Master Westlake." Mary-Beth placed his food in front of him. Mother and Father were gone. His sister was dressed as a bank teller might.

Gilbert hummed a tune he could not place, one that suddenly flowed through him. The melody was bright and inquisitive, as if building away from a question and into a final answer. Sunlight illuminated the steam rising from his plate. Pulling out his journal, Gilbert flipped to the first empty page and wrote: BREAKFAST: SCRAMBLED EGGS, BACON, FRIED POTATOES. Logging, for Gilbert, was a trick of repetition he and Mary-Beth worked out in the beginning. The Reruns were her idea, as were the daily notations. After two years, she didn't have to bother him to write things down. Gilbert closed his book and began shoveling eggs into his mouth.

Mary-Beth sat across from him.

"Gilbert," Mary-Beth said. She opened his Rerun to the pink Post-it. "Read from here."

Gilbert gathered another large bite of food into his mouth. In handwriting he recognized as his own, he read aloud from the journal: "'This week is the last we will spend in our home. I am sad to leave, but I'll be happier at Springfield's Cognitive Institute and Recovery Center.' An asylum? You're putting me away."

"1439, *asylum,* place of refuge, sanctuary," Mary-Beth said. She beamed at recalling this answer from *Strike Zone*. "Greek *asylos,* safe from violence."

"1776, English." Gilbert said, "Institute of special care, as in for the insane or orphaned."

"Come on, Gil," she said. "From your first appearance on the show? The *Strike Zone* Challenge Question that sent you to the next round. Asylum!"

"I do remember," Gilbert said. "Barbara was my first competitor. From Omaha, Nebraska. Age forty-three. Brown hair, brown eyes. She lost on the word obfuscate—"

Interrupting him, Mary-Beth tapped the Rerun with her finger. "Read on, please."

"'I am happy that Mary-Beth is in love. Twyla has nice hair and is not the Homo-erectus I once thought her to be. She is a nice woman who loves my sister very much.'"

He looked up from his reading. "You've eloped with an australopithecine?"

"Be nice, please."

"Truth is often revealed through the negative," Gilbert said.

Gilbert closed the journal and moved it to the side of his plate. Mary-Beth had not eaten any of her food. Her eyes followed his every move, and she smiled in a sad way that annoyed Gilbert. He stopped chewing; a ball of meal-paste stuffed to the side of his cheek.

"I'd appreciate it if you did not watch me eat," he said. "I will not relieve your guilt pertaining to my looming incarceration."

He put down his fork and turned away from Mary-Beth. The window was open and dead moths cluttered the screen. Mother's empty vase sat next to a plate of half-eaten food. Gilbert picked up his journal in order to notate breakfast and recited the scientific and common names for moths under his breath: "Parnassians, *Papilionidae*; Sulphurs, *Pieridae*; Metalmarks, *Riodinidae*; Wild Silk, *Saturniidae*—"

When she realized Gilbert's memory had hiccupped, Mary-Beth covered her face with a napkin to hide her tears. She cried even though she was happy. At that moment, Twyla was painting the living room yellow, and she thought about surprising her with coffee and biscuits.

"I have to leave the house for a few hours," she said. "Please, Gil, box your things. There isn't much. The Brain is all put away—"

"My closet?"

Gilbert kept nearly twenty years' worth of Reruns, photos, newspaper clippings, and letters in the closet. Every birthday, as per ritual, he combed through it all and notated surprising events on a voice recorder and listened to his life the first of every month throughout the year.

He left the kitchen flustered, forgetting his Rerun on the table.

Mary-Beth called after him. "Goddamnit, Gil! You helped."

A yellow Post-it was taped to the banister at the foot of the stairs: DON'T FORGET TO PACK. Another, at the top of the stairs, said the same thing. There were other notes in the hallway: TURN OFF THE LIGHT. FLUSH THE TOILET. BRUSH YOUR TEETH.

In his room, boxes lined the walls. Some were empty and tagged with Post-its that told him what went where: CLOTHES. MISC. MOTH AND BUTTERFLY COLLECTION.

On his lampshade, a Post-it read: TURN OFF LIGHT. Another said: TAKE OFF SOCKS (in his handwriting). His closet had been emptied of every ordered stack of memory, each labeled by year, and color-coded: Events (holidays, birthdays), Outings, Meals, Letters, and Photos.

He shut his eyes and tried to recall The Brain's order— stacks of ledgers and colored file folders—but all he saw were the cedar walls and open closet door.

Next to his nightstand, a plastic binder was anchored to the wall by a length of chain. Photos of Gilbert in a chronological order were arranged on the cover. YOUR LIFE was written in blue marker.

The first three pages contained a typed letter written by Mary-Beth and laminated. He found more photographs of himself from boyhood to present. In the earlier photos, he was plump around the middle but had skinny arms and legs. By the time he reached the final photo labeled aged thirty-two, his body had fully succumbed to pear-shape. Mary-Beth had tagged the progression [YEAR (AGE)]. He flipped between photos that showed a boy with curly long hair [1975 (7)] and the man whose bald crown reflected a camera flash [2000 (32)]. The boy he could place, but he did not recognize the aging man.

> DEAR GIL:
>
> IT'S ME, MARY-BETH, BUT WHO ELSE WOULD IT BE, RIGHT? I MEAN NAME ONE OTHER PERSON BESIDES ME. PEOPLE FROM THE PAST DON'T COUNT, GILBERT. THAT'S THE POINT OF THIS BOOK, OF YOUR RERUNS, OF THE BRAIN. IT'S ALL SO YOU CAN KEEP TABS ON YOUR LIFE. IT'S BEEN TWO YEARS NOW, AND I DON'T THINK YOUR MEMORY IS COMING BACK. THIS IS TO TELL YOU WHAT HAPPENED. YOU HAD A SEIZURE BECAUSE TUMORS WERE CROWDING YOUR BRAIN. THEY HAD TO REMOVE THEM OR YOU'D DIE. YOU MIGHT HAVE DIED FROM THE SURGERY, BUT WHAT CHOICE DID I HAVE? I SIGNED FOR IT, SO I GUESS IT'S MY FAULT. BUT YOU'RE ALIVE! THEY HAD TO TAKE OUT YOUR HIPPOCAMPUS. THE DOCTOR SEEMED CERTAIN YOU'D RECOVER, BUT WITHOUT THE LITTLE SEA HORSE LOOKING THINGS, YOU'LL NEVER MAKE NEW MEMORIES AGAIN.

From outside, a loud crash. Gilbert placed the binder back on his nightstand and watched Mary-Beth wedge small boxes in the bed of her Toyota pickup. Red tape covered a broken taillight and the passenger door was spray-painted gray. Gilbert thought this very tacky, but so like Mary-Beth. She climbed into the truck, and with an explosion of black exhaust, she pulled away.

Mary-Beth throws a sheet over the TV screen and turns the sound down low so only she can hear. Gilbert plugs his ears for extra protection. Because Gilbert has memorized the structure of every aired episode of Strike Zone, *he devised this study plan. Combing through VHS tapes, Mary-Beth picks questions at random.*

"Pteropus giganteus?"

"Flying fox, better known as the fruit bat. From the Pteropidae *family.*"

Mary-Beth fast-forwards to a new segment.

"Who are the Matabele?"

"South African Bantu tribe," he says. "Matabele is a European corruption of the true word, Ndebele, which means hidden people because of the giant rhinoceros hides warriors walked behind when entering battle."

"What is the common name for Mangelwurzel?"

"Mangelwurzel?" Gilbert asks. "Pet names for your privates will not help me to win."

"Beets, Gil," she says. "A giant beet."

"It's 2:59," Gilbert says, saddened that he didn't know the answer. "Westerns."

Mary-Beth removes the sheet, and turns on Gun Smoke. *A band of outlaws ride over a hill of poverty grass. Dust clouds hover around the men as they stop to survey the frontier town below. Black horses pull a covered wagon down Main Street.*

A mattress without a frame sat on the floor, bare of any bedding. This was not his room. There were no curtains and a heavy-limbed and leafless tree outside the window dimmed the midday sun. Boxes lined the wall, taped closed and labeled: LINEN, CLOTHES, DVDS.

A TV lay face down on the floor.

The only box not shut had the words GILBERT'S PRIVATE THINGS written in purple. Gilbert panicked at the sight of his name in an unfamiliar room. He would have told himself about any day trips if he were meant to leave the house, and he reached for his Rerun, but found nothing. His memory-journal was missing. He hiccupped. One followed the other in such rapid succession he could not catch his breath. He closed his eyes and recited entries from *Britannica*, 1954—"Heart beat: seventy per minute; four thousand two hundred an hour; one hundred thousand eight hundred a day; thirty-six million seven hundred and ninety-two thousand a year. Blood circulates through twelve thousand miles of blood ways."

Breathing normally again, he opened the box with his name.

Besides a collection of VHS tapes (GIL ON *STRIKE ZONE*) there was a padded manila envelope labeled DO NOT TOUCH. It was obviously meant for him. It bore his name. He ripped the glued clasp open and pulled out one undated Rerun. Stuffed halfway through the journal was an official release form for $187,000 made out to him but signed by Mary-Beth. The journal was blank except for the first ten pages. He flipped to the final page and read his handwriting: DON'T TRUST ANYONE. NOT THE LAWYER, MR. DUBESKI; HE'S IN ON IT. SO IS THE BANK TELLER. ~~I KNEW SOMETHING~~ MARY-BETH'S A LIAR.

Another slip of paper fell from the journal. Bending low to pick it up, he noticed the letterhead: *STRIKE ZONE*™.

DEAR MR. WESTLAKE,

WE REGRET THE TRAGIC CIRCUMSTANCES THAT ENDED YOUR SOARING SUCCESS ON *STRIKE ZONE*™. THOUGH YOUR WINNINGS WILL BE HONORED, WE CANNOT OFFER YOU THE $80,000 WON DURING *STRIKE ZONE CHALLENGE*™, AS YOU DID NOT PROPERLY FINISH THIS SECTION OF THE CONTEST. HOWEVER, IN ACCORDANCE WITH THE GAME SHOW ASSOCIATION ETHICS AGREEMENT YOUR REMAINING $187,000 IS YOURS TO KEEP. AS ILLINOIS STATE LAW DEMANDS, WE CANNOT RELEASE ANY FUNDS UNTIL A VALID SIGNATURE AUTHORIZES THE WINNINGS INTO YOUR NAME.

PLEASE SIGN, DATE THE FORMS ENCLOSED, AND RETURN PROMPTLY.

SINCERELY,

ASSOCIATE PRODUCER, DEBORAH HOFSTADTER

"Tragic," he said. "1545, Latin *tragicus*, from Greek *tragikos*. From *tagos*, goat, or a satyr impersonated by a goat singer."

Money? He wondered how long Mary-Beth had hidden this from him. If only he could talk to Charlie Weathers, tell him his sister was a liar and had no right to sign this form then surely, he'd get the winnings owed to him. On a clean page, he wrote FIND MR. WEATHERS, and he added the address of the TV studio at 1546 Front Street taken from the letterhead.

He slipped the journal into his back pocket and stepped out into the hallway.

He holds one Challenger flight wing tight against the shuttle and waits for the model-glue to settle. But a crash followed by his sister's irritating laugh causes him to tense and the wing snaps. He gives up on gluing together his model, once he realizes Mary-Beth has no intention of turning down the country music blaring from her room. She has been holed up with her friend Liana for hours.

He sneaks across the hall carrying a glass of water, opens Mary-Beth's door, and tosses the full glass blindly towards his sister's bed. Quickly, he presses his body flat against the outer wall. He waits for the girls to shriek. When nothing happens, he peeks inside. Mary-Beth kneels between Liana's naked legs. The water didn't reach them, but instead landed on the floor amidst charcoal prints of Liana's face.

Liana raises from the pillow—the music pounding—and screams when she sees Gilbert in the doorway.

Liana disappeared after that and Mary-Beth only left her room at night. Gilbert regularly caught her sneaking out and coming back home with bags of fast food or video rentals.

"I'm agoraphobic, Gil," she said when he questioned her. "Leave me alone or I might become xenophobic, too."

"Xeno is Greek for stranger. So, you'd have to become an amnesiac for that to pan out."

"Mom swears you don't have autism," she said. "But I mean, like, really?"

"I'm curious," he said.

Gilbert looked for Liana after their parents died, but she wasn't at the funeral. Irises, dandelions, and lilies surrounded the open grave, and men in mud-stained coveralls lowered a double casket into the ground.

Gilbert was bothered by the lack of variation in the tune he hummed. He expected a turn, as with poetry, a dactyl or anapest, to break the iambic bounce, but no change occurred. For a moment, he tried to block out all else and recall the origin of the theme forever stuck in his head, but his concentration was quickly drowned by a thumping rhythm. He was not home but at a store. A gas station with cigarettes and bottles of liquor behind the counter. A man was coming toward him, a man with hair greased and stuck to his pale cheeks, a man with aberrantly long nails that hooked downward from his fingers, a man who knew his name.

"Gilbert? You shouldn't be down here without Mary-Beth."

He had nearly touched Gil, reaching for his shirtsleeve; he had nearly scraped him with those witchy nails, but Gilbert ran to the far end of the store and yelled for help. The cretin stopped his assault then, stood where he was, and watched Gilbert with a blatant look of annoyance.

"I'll call Mary-Beth. Get her to deal with you."

"What do you know about Mary-Beth. Who are you?"

"I'm the same jerk that has worked this corner market for ten lousy years and in that time, you've called the cops on me, I don't know, fifteen times. Look: I'm Gary. You know me and your sister knows me. And I know you ain't got no memory so I'm sorry for coming at you like that, but Mary-Beth asked me to keep an eye out for you today. Said you'd probably act out considering the move." The man, Gary, dialed and spoke into the phone. Gilbert listened as he told Mary-Beth to come get him, said, "Gilbert's spazzing out in the store."

Gilbert took out his Rerun and looked it over for a clue as to why he was in this store in the first place. He had no money, no wallet, or anything else in his pockets besides the journal. He felt a panic, something darker than fear of this man's claws, when he read about Mary-Beth's theft. Gary couldn't be trusted.

"Well," Gary said. "I'll try. I mean what am I supposed to do with him, play truth or dare? Look. He's back by the beer cave. Maybe I can lock up until you get here. Maybe I'll get him loaded as punishment for your negligence. I'm kidding, kidding—"

Gilbert ran then, ran through the door and out into a parking lot that smelled of gasoline and tar and garbage. There was a man in a red car, a man who had just pulled up and had yet to shut off the engine and Gilbert ran to him, yelling, "Help! Help!"

Mary-Beth refuses to get in the cab because it is numbered 0013. The cab smells of something sweet and spiced.

"Ride in a cursed cab if you want," she says. "It's your big day."

Gilbert leans in, "1546 Front?"

"You're the genius boy!" the driver says. "Good luck today," he says. "Final Four!"

There is a picture of Ganesha, the elephant-headed Hindu god, taped to the center console and a lit stick of incense burns in the ashtray. Ganesh is the Lord of Beginnings and Remover of Obstacles. A fortuitous sign, Gilbert thinks.

In the dressing room, make-up artists and designers rush around Gilbert. They powder his face, adding rouge, eyeliner, and lipstick. They strip him down to his briefs and then dress him in a sea-foam green suit that shines when the light hits. It fits too tight around his stomach, and though he complains, the beauticians just coo about how handsome he looks.

"When do I get to meet Mr. Weathers?" he asks a girl with feathered hair and bell-bottoms like Mary-Beth wears.

She laughs. "On stage, honey."

"I wanted to thank him."

A woman he hasn't seen before walks in. "Save it for the camera," she says, and makes notes on her clipboard. She harries the designers. "Showtime in ten minutes," she says. "Got it everyone? I want boy-genius to go last but make sure he looks like a finale instead of the caboose!"

Gilbert catches sight of himself in the mirror. He has never liked to linger on his reflection but now that his face is masked in make-up, he can't turn away from the chubby boy in bright colors peering back.

Because he knew from the smell and shape of the vehicle's interior that it was not Mary-Beth's truck, he was afraid to look toward the driver's seat. Gilbert's notebook lay open on his lap. He read: DRIVER IS DAN. He sighed and smiled at Dan.

"Not a talker, huh? Me? I'm an open man. Got nothing to lose, so got nothing to hide. Hell, I'm free!" Dan laughed from deep in his throat.

"Sometimes I don't recall things very well," Gilbert said. "I write them down."

"What you write about me?"

"That you are Dan."

"Put down some other stuff. Like, Dan is handsome, young, virile, and any *mamacita* would want to *fiesta* in his Cancun hotel room." Dan laughed again and tapped an off-beat rhythm on the steering wheel. His chin was lost to a pouch of fleshy skin.

Gilbert didn't write down any of these things.

"Why you heading downtown?"

"IBTV Studios," Gil said. "I need to see Charlie Weathers."

"*Strike Zone*?"

"I'm a contestant," Gilbert said.

"They bringing that show back? This one time me and my buddy Doug smoked weed in his mom's basement and *Strike Zone* came on and we were blasted man and all of the sudden a contestant, this weird kid, I mean spooky smart, just fell out on stage. Boom. Started shaking and drooling; they cut to commercial, and Dougie stood up and put his hand over his heart and recited the pledge of allegiance, and I joined him too, and we were quiet and the basement was quiet, and get this man: I could hear my heart beating in my ears. Never happened since, but I swear it was like some kind of stoned empathy man. I was feeling all the blood rush and fear that kid was feeling when he collapsed."

Gilbert imagined a dark bedsheet falling over a boy on stage. The sheet reached his body and covered him from the bright studio lights until he was only a lumped shape on the floor.

"Show hasn't been on for at least a decade, man." Dan said.

Gilbert had never imagined a world without *Strike Zone*. "What year is it now?"

"2000. Y2K. The end times! What cave have you been in?"

Gilbert wrote: 2000.

Outside Gilbert's window, farms morphed into stretches of new and identical houses with plotted yards. He liked how they were divided into squares but arranged in oval divisions. Some had pools in the shape of kidney beans that sparkled green in the sunshine.

The downtown buildings didn't have the same gleam he remembered. They were dull, unwashed. Some were abandoned. Dan pulled in front of a dilapidated high-rise and cut the ignition.

"Where are we?" Gilbert asked.

"IBTV," Dan said. "The lion fountain used to be right there." Dan pointed out two construction dumpsters full of broken furniture. "Man, I loved that fountain."

Gilbert walked in between the dumpsters. A *Strike Zone* emblem—a circle with a lightning bolt shooting horizontal—was set in the concrete. This was where the bronze children played, he recalled. A plaque read: STRIKE ZONE™ APRIL 1975—JUNE 1985. It was dark between the dumpsters. Hot.

After he exhausts all translations of dark, Gilbert lists the variations of blackbird under his breath. Behind the desk hangs a photo of Mr. Dubeski with Papa at the symphony. Papa holds a violin against his chest while Mr. Dubeski gives a thumbs up to the camera. Heavy drapes cover the windows of the lawyer's office. John Dubeski—Gilbert's god-father, and Papa's oldest friend. Gilbert wears his favorite outfit of plaid pants and a Hawaiian shirt. Mary-Beth looks like a hobo in her army coat, scuffed bell-bottoms, and sunglasses on in a dark room.

"Mary-Beth," Mr. Dubeski says. "Sue and I can take him. You don't have to do this."

"He stays home," she says. "He'll be eighteen in three months. Practically legal. Look. I found him hiding in the attic insulation when I mentioned he might leave home. He was screaming the whole time I dragged him out about how it was his fault."

"No one could've anticipated the events. Black ice is common in Chicago, common as the high winds. If that semi hadn't been there, they'd have slid into a field."

"But they were driving to see him at the studio. He remembers this. I think it's one of his last memories."

"How will you provide? If I agree that is."

"Don't know," she says. "Get a job. Live off our parents' life insurance. Who cares!?"

"I care," Mr. Dubeski says.

"John," she says. "I promise to take good care of him."

A beige station wagon was parked under the bright fluorescence near the pumps. A man with greased black hair that hung over his face and delicately long nails watched Gilbert from the entrance of the gas station. The tune he hummed varied greatly from the bass-driven pop music on the stereo. Gilbert did not recognize the woman filling her tank.

"Can you tell me where I am, please?"

"Gil." When Gilbert didn't respond, the woman said, "Already, Gil?"

He liked being called Gil. Charlie Weathers called him Gil. But this woman laughed in a way that hurt Gilbert and so did the edge of frustration in her voice when she said, "Well, Gil. You're at Shell off Exit 1B." She gestured to the highway.

Gilbert thanked her. She honked three times and drove away, leaving Gilbert alone near the pumps. The man appeared again, watching Gilbert from the doorway to the store, which made him nervous and so he walked to the edge of the lot and studied the insects attracted to the lights. It was dusk and insects sought warmth among the blue-white streetlamps, throwing their bodies into the light, clinging and dying all in a flurry.

Gilbert watched the steady stream of traffic move along the highway in both directions and counted all red vehicles he saw. He counted fifteen before Mary-Beth pulled up.

"Get in."

When they were safely on the highway, driving in the opposite direction of their childhood home, she threw a Rerun onto Gilbert's lap.

"Found it on the kitchen table."

Gilbert located his recent entry, a breakfast log.

"Give me the other one. The one you have on you."

When Gilbert handed her the Rerun he'd been writing in all that day, she tossed it out of her window. "This can never happen, again. Okay? I'm stupid for not burning this damn thing sooner. Truth is, I did take your money. I spent it on our bills and food, but I also bought this truck, drank most of it. But I paid you back half by now, and that's how you're moving to that institute. Twyla and I will kick in for your monthlies, but that's it baby brother. No more guilt."

"Why did you throw out my journal?"

She eyed him. After all these years, she still couldn't tell when he was lucid and when he had lost the thread.

"Do you recall the alphabet game?" Gilbert asked. "We played it on road trips with Papa and Mother."

They passed a green exit sign and Mary-Beth called out, "Applewood Drive!"

Gilbert searched the endless corn and soy farms, waiting for his sign, but as they tunneled down the interstate deeper into the Chicago suburbs he saw none, neither off-ramps, nor ads, just an endless progression of the same landscape recycling itself with each new silo or barn or lone tree in the mass of night-gray fields.

Gilbert saw a blue streak of lightning across the sky and a familiar song he could not place popped into his head. A hunger seized him, a deep hunger, as if he hadn't eaten anything all day.

"So, we're going out for dinner?"

"I thought we might eat over at my new place, Gil. With Twyla," Mary-Beth said.

"Let's go to Bennie's instead. You shouldn't have any cheeseburgers though. The way you've put on weight. Perhaps seafood. Lobster or a crab platter?"

Mary-Beth laughed, and the pressure that had built up in her body now forcefully exhaled. She laughed until all the tension released from her lungs. "Yes," she said to her brother. "Yes," she said. "Fish is fine. Fish sounds great."

LUZ

Luz and George were fucking the first time he saw the new neighbor, *not* making love, no, to make love one needed some semblance of foreplay, an act the two often neglected. Neither preferred doggy-style, but ever since *Bastion Hill* won an American Soap Award and George was promoted to head writer, Luz had refused any other way; he hated how George stared down at him with this self-satisfied look and besides, George complained that kneeling hurt his back—everything else came easily for George, after all.

Luz watched the thin man run his fingers along the windowsill inside what had been, at least since Luz had moved into George's second home in Asheville, a reliably empty apartment. Luz was transfixed and George noticed the change, the body now cold with distraction.

George plopped down on the bed, sweating heavily. Before George could say anything, ask questions—"Where did you go? Where do you always go?"—Luz pulled on a velour robe and went to the bathroom for a shower.

When he returned, George stood in a pair of jogging pants at the bedroom window. "Neighbors?"

"People move out and people move in," Luz said. "If we were crustaceans, we'd have new neighbors each time the moon finished a cycle."

"Is that true?" George asked. "Do crustaceans float with the tide?"

Luz didn't know if this was true or not, but enjoyed the reckless image of crabs scattering along the ocean floor.

"I fly to the city at nine," George said. "How about Indian food?"

Luz pulled on a pair of cotton underwear that belonged to an ex. They were thick with holes around the waistband and felt utilitarian in a way that made him want to work for long hours. This, the house and allowance, was his time to produce something great. Too many years had been spent distracted by romance, distracted by frail egos of previous lovers, and Luz didn't want to squander the security George offered. A balance had to be struck between black lace and white cotton.

"No eating out tonight," Luz said.

"I rescued you from that dive so we could spend more time together," George said.

Luz paused midway into pulling on a pair of track pants and crossed his eyes, pushed out his bottom jaw and aped George— *Me. Strongman. Rescue.* Luz had expected him to be more mature, but at forty-three George was as childish as all the others. George ignored the rebuke and watched as the apartment manager, dressed in a security uniform and utility belt, wrestled a mattress through the front door.

"I really hate that guy," George said.

A month prior, George had been in a short-tempered mood after flying to Asheville from New York when the manager came at him waving a Maglite and clicking his tongue because George had parked in front of the complex. George threatened to *kick the shit out of* the manager but ended up face down against the hood of his BMW.

"Don't let him see you prying."

"I'm not prying," George said. "Just fascinated."

Luz hated the way he said *fascinated*. Every time he used *that* tone with *that* word, something from their lives ended up on *Bastion Hill.*

Luz retreated to the studio—a small bedroom that had been transformed into a workspace. Two lofts were anchored to the walls five feet from the floor and red velvet closed off each platform. The worktable was a clay-strewn mess; a twelve-inch marionette of Luz dangled from a hook in the ceiling: ball cap cocked at an angle, ratty polo with a stencil of Trump's face covered in pie, and black jeans rolled above a pair of hiking boots. Even before quitting Café Troubadour in Brooklyn, George having offered to support him, Luz only worked at night. He needed absolute control over lighting, and the sun was a fickle beast. While filming one frame at a time for an animation, any shift in shadow strobed through the scene as spectral blacks. Luz only had two months before his installation was set to open and could not afford much interference or mistakes. The stages for the current animation were simple enough, a Victorian dollhouse positioned among papier-mâché cornfields, cows, and a dairy barn. Various painted backdrops for close-ups: a willow tree, a pond, and a tractor. Mother and Father and all nine O'Brien siblings had both miniature and large puppets with moveable limbs and interchangeable faces, though Mother and Father rarely needed any other face besides hard and observant. It was the story within the story of this animation of the Iowa dairy farm where Luz grew up that stumped him. At first, Luz was driven by memory of home: the elongated beauty of farms and flat earth, the wind and walls of snow in winter. He simply wanted to relive the landscape. But when he thought of his brothers and sisters, all still in Anamosa, the art turned inward, and Luz no longer knew which story to tell. Midwestern expanse was all so confining, especially for a queer in Catholic country. Luz's family was sober and reticent when Luz visited. He'd left home years before, first moving to Iowa City and then to Chicago, then to St. Paul, to Montreal, to Asheville, where Luz's only friend from home, Jo Ann, lived, to Brooklyn where he earned a very expensive film degree at NYU, and finally, back to Asheville where George owned this summer condo. How to tell the story of living in rural Iowa without also dipping into the bottomless narratives created by leaving Iowa?

Luz caught sight of the neighbor carrying a suitcase in each hand, a shoulder bag in the crook of an elbow. The windows of George's flat perfectly mirrored that of the stranger's across the alley. He reminded Luz of a lodger from film noir, a villain maybe, the way he stood politely aside while the manager flipped the light switch on and then off again. The neighbor had a strong jaw, but a thin waist and wrists, like puppet joints. What attracted Luz was the way he moved, languid strides from door to window, looking down into the alley and then up towards the sky where Luz knew the crows sat in gossiping threes and fours: there was something equally masculine and feminine about this muscular white man with a goatee and crew cut whose hips pivoted to the left and pelvis jutted forward when he turned to bid farewell. Luz could mime these movements perfectly were he to sculpt a marionette of the neighbor. Strangely, the neighbor's walk and eyes were as driving and sharp as Mother's. Mother: broad shouldered, scowling, and silent. Was this man maternal, or was Mother manly? The neighbor caught sight of Luz. His eyes widened, and he held the stare. Luz did not know for how long the man had looked at him this way.

Luz waved; the neighbor lowered his blinds.

In the living room, Luz found George stretched out on his back on the floor.

"Do you think Robin would slum it?" George asked. "You know, someone outside of *Bastion Hill*, like a rock star or club owner." Robin was George's prize character—the moderately attractive rebellious teen that hated the wealth she was born into. The rest of George's cast indulged in normal business—attempted murder, adultery, and prodigal sons returned home from Hawaii. Robin's millennial pithiness and distraction gave *Bastion Hill* an edge.

"Our new neighbor just brought in suitcases."

George sat up. "How's he look?"

"Handsome. Chiseled. Gay. Maybe?"

"Is he black? The network wouldn't do interracial, but a rapper maybe."

"You sound racist."

"It's not me. It's the network."

"Okay. Then you sound like a complicit racist."

"And you're an expert?" George sulked. "How many non-white friends do you have?"

Luz only had one friend, Jo Ann, and she was white, like, Iowa-white, and of course, there was George, who was Jewish, non-practicing. When Luz fucked George, he always cried *Harder, Goy!* Luz never really liked this role, the goy-bully role. Normally, he loved strapping on a dick. But George went somewhere beyond the sex with this role, and then George always sulked after, feeling let down because the more he willed Luz to violence, the more Luz felt tenderness and care.

The next morning, Monday, Luz got out of bed at 10:30. George was gone and would not return until Thursday night or later. Sometimes he had to skip weekends. Besides *Bastion Hill,* George supervised a secondary open-serial, *Laurel Canyon*—an upbeat drama about life after college in a small Colorado town—a show that Luz once followed religiously. Being head-writer meant more time in New York, which meant less time Luz spent crippled by self-doubt. Luz loved the alone time, the monastic patterns of work and rest and meals and, most of all, his morning run.

Luz took off down Haywood and jogged towards Montford Cemetery. The stoplights at the three-way intersection in front of St. Lawrence's Basilica had fritzed again and appeared downcast darkened above deadlocked traffic. Cars and delivery trucks jerked forward, nose to tail, grimy exhaust was visible in the air but the heat had yet to build and did not tamper the luscious breeze. Luz quickly left the shit-show behind and within minutes clicked into a zone. He had dreamt about Wally. The vision, a memory: Luz had lost his virginity to Wally, an act Jo Ann said didn't count because Luz had not been penetrated, such Catholic wording, but had instead worn a strap-on. Wally, a freckled boy of sixteen who had never hidden his infatuation with Freddy Prince Jr. was so eager for the experience, Luz recalled. Luz hadn't known what type of sex he desired, not like Wally had known, but when Wally asked Luz to fuck him, suddenly, Luz had never wanted anything more in his young life. Wally was still in Iowa, Luz realized, working at Game Pros in the Coralville Mall. *What does fucking Wally say about home?* For so long now he had lived out in the open as queer. In his heart and mind, he was not a *woman*, as his biology suggested, but undoubtedly male. If he *must* choose, if he had to categorize himself, then he was a gay man, butch for sure. But that's it isn't it, Luz thought, the crux: the O'Briens knew nothing of Luz, and Luz had so purposefully maintained this mystification that Mother sent Christmas and birthday cards that read *To My Precious Daughter.* Home was a fantasy. What did it matter if Mother and Father and the O'Brien siblings knew Luz's heart? Luz had chosen secrecy and exile as opposed to welcoming the family's fear and bigotry. As a pitch for the animation, however, this synopsis would end with a sentimental question like *but at what cost?* Luz thought: *The coming out story is overdone. I hate protest film.* But that was what made the story so hard to tell: it was impossible to separate queerness from coming of age, from home, from George, from the simple pleasure of a morning jog. Wally knew even before Luz did; Wally knew Luz would say yes.

On the way back to George's, Luz passed the corner complex and saw the new neighbor. He was shirtless in the small lawn, carrying a box of potted plants. Luz smiled, the neighbor stared, and Luz felt the man's eyes follow him when he rounded the corner toward home, unsettled now by a familiar anxiety. He knew the feeling well, it was akin to remorse but at least for the moment, Luz thought, he had nothing to regret.

In the studio, Luz peeled his shirt away and felt the sweat cool against his chest and neck. Luz was in the habit of working topless, and as he rolled clay into a ball for Wally's face, he purposefully stood at the window. Luz giggled; the man was downstairs and would not catch him, but he wanted the neighbor to appear. When he did not, a depression took the place of playfulness. Luz grabbed a dry shirt and slipped it over his damp torso, leaving the unformed face, oval and wanting, on the workbench.

It was then, standing in the doorway that Luz decided to sneak into the neighbor's apartment. Empty pots and two bags of soil, various aspidistras still in plastic sheaths had surrounded the neighbor outside. What were the chances of him returning to his apartment? Luz could not enter through the front. Perhaps there was a fire exit? George's condo was new, decked out with evacuation routes that led through the laundry and exercise rooms, but the neighboring complex was old and run-down. It was worth it to look for a back entrance, even if it was locked. His joy returned with the anticipation of danger.

Luz walked close to the condo's exterior, stepping softly past the alley until he came to a steel door at the rear of the neighboring complex. There was no key code, as Luz suspected, and it opened with a turn of the knob. Why allow for such coincidence if not for a reason? Up the flight of stairs, first loft on the right— as George's would have been the first on the left—and yet another game of fate. The neighbor's door stood slightly ajar.

Breathless. Luz imagined the evening ahead, how restful everything would feel after breaking the rules, how calm after the high of evasion.

Inside, Luz found a clean and sparsely furnished home in a palette of grays and blues offset by a large area rug with random orange arrows shooting across a full moon. What looked like a shrine beneath the window was set inside of a large vegetable crate and covered with votive candles arranged on white taffeta was a photograph of a drag queen; her wig, a bouffant. She towered on stage in six-inch stilettos and wore a wedding gown. Luz fumbled for his smartphone, shaking; his fingers hitting the wrong digits for the access code. He took one photo and then a second. He heard movement, but it was his own.

Sitting at the kitchen table, Luz spread out prints of the two pictures taken at the neighbor's apartment. This, he believed, was the real animation and not Iowa at all: the story behind this shrine, the story of the neighbor and the drag queen. Luz could see it play out perfectly on screen: begin with the shrine and the photo, have the queen, Mitzy—that's what Luz will call her—break from the photo and begin to dance. Something slow at first, something with hips and breasts swiveling that transitions into something upbeat, like "I Will Survive." Irony. Yes, she doesn't survive, does she? Killed in the 80s, a darker time for genderqueers. And the neighbor— vengeful and love-worn—kills the man who left Mitzy's body near a dumpster. A marionette of Mitzy will dance the entire time, while a live-action film of the events will play on a little screen, an iPhone perhaps, back of stage but center. It was insane to change plans so soon to the opening, but nothing moved with the Iowa-film, just stills of nature, the sound of weather.

George appeared and nuzzled the nape of Luz's neck, his fingers sliding down Luz's shirt, as he pinched, and tugged Luz's nipples. Luz pulled George's hand away and kissed his wrist, a simple gesture to curb the sting of rejection.

"Going out for drinks with Nate. He's in town doing a commercial at Biltmore."

"I'll probably be asleep when you get back. Wake me if you want."

"If only I could wake you now."

"You sound like one of your characters," Luz said. *"Meh-meh-meh-meh."*

"Oh right. I'm a creative black hole?"

"Creative black hole is a little dramatic. More like... creative display case."

"Commedia Del Arte, babe" he said. "Been around since the Greeks. What are you working on anyhow? Who's the queen?"

Luz gathered his pictures and pushed passed George. "No one. Just something I pulled off the internet."

In the studio, Luz stuffed the prints at the very back of his desk drawer. He wasn't ready to share Mitzy yet, especially not with George. Wally's puppet lay along the table next to a crowd of various faces and hands, the black dildo in miniature, his bed with an Apollo Shuttle headboard waiting for a coat of paint. Luz studied the puppet of Wally, changing out various faces: one bright and eager, one afraid, one happy. He worked mindlessly sewing clothes for Wally and a bedspread with spaceships and the moon for Wally's bed. He gave up at eleven, cut all lights but for a miniature lamp in the Iowa-house. Luz uncorked a Pinot Noir from the wine cabinet and brought the bottle back into the studio. George had finally gone out, and Luz studied the pictures he'd taken of the neighbor's shrine.

The neighbor stood at his window, suddenly, fiercely. He stared across the alley into the studio. Luz brought down a marionette of his own likeness and waltzed along the workbench toward the window. He had the puppet wave, but the neighbor did not move or avert his hard gaze. It was as if he did not see either puppet or puppeteer. Luz finished the glass of wine in one gulp and poured another. The neighbor's gaze was set at some fixed point in front of the window where Luz knew the shrine was displayed. With his hands cupped together, the neighbor knelt and rocked back and forth, his head shaking out *nonononono*. It was true. Mitzy had been killed, Luz thought. The neighbor had killed. Luz moved closer to the window as if proximity might illuminate or deepen his understanding of the neighbor, of the queen in the shrine. Luz felt an urge to comfort, to hold him and kiss him, just as the neighbor stood and walked out of sight. Luz picked paint from his overalls, glancing toward the neighbor's apartment. He turned on the over-head and the outside vanished—all he could see now was his own reflection in the lighted window.

When George came home, Luz lay awake reading. Without brushing his teeth, George crawled in next to him and lazily tugged at his waistband.

"How was your night?" George asked. He smelled of cigarettes.

"You smoked."

George rolled on top of Luz, crushing the book to his chest; his legs flat beneath George's weight. He kissed Luz's neck and then his mouth. Luz kissed him back, but weakly.

"George," Luz said, pushing his shoulders away.

George kissed down from his neck to his chest.

"You're so beautiful," he said.

"Serious about the rain check, George. You're drunk, and I'm tired." Luz pushed him off, and George rolled over onto his side.

"Don't I give you enough?" he said to the wall, sounding like he might cry. That happened sometimes, when George had too much to drink, he cried.

"You give me plenty, but I'm not a robot and can't put out whenever."

"Not an even trade," he said.

"Didn't realize we were bartering."

George responded with a watery snore.

Hours later, Luz still couldn't sleep. A car passed on the street below causing light to float across the room. The neighbor's apartment was dark.

The following weekend, Luz cut his morning run short by half an hour and when he entered the condo, he found George masturbat-ing to porn. George knelt on a couch pillow, his pants down to his ankles, and in the split second before George slammed the laptop shut, Luz saw the actors: one man, older and pudgy sucking the cock of a "she-male," as the genre was so irritatingly named, with massive silicone breasts. Flustered, George didn't try to stand or even move position. He looked over his shoulder, pouting before Luz had a chance to say anything.

"I don't care, George. I like porn sometimes. I like facials. I sometimes sink into despair over this desire to cum without regard on your face, George, because it can't happen. I watch those compilations. Second after second of different penises and different faces—"

"Please, stop. You're making it worse."

"Unless you wish I had—"

"Just stop, Luz," George stood, his face flushed as he pulled up his bottoms. "I don't like porn. I wanted to cum, okay? I wanted to cum without bothering you."

"Oh."

Luz drove a box of body parts down to the public kiln. It wasn't enough to justify his own burn, and so he called Jo Ann and she agreed to throw in. Luz hadn't left the apartment in four days. He had sculpted three new heads for the neighbor's queen, attempting to capture the fierceness and beauty based on the stolen photographs, but it was frustrating. No matter how much work Luz put into the puppets, there was always something missing, something he feared could only be realized if he had access to the real thing.

Jo Ann loafed around the studio lobby; she was a squat woman with a bowl cut that made her whole being resemble a Soviet-bloc tenement. Unlike Luz's paltry shoebox of ceramics, Jo Ann had three crates full and stacked on a dolly.

"Too busy giving it up to the ol' man?" Jo Ann pointed to Luz's box and thrust her pelvis like a hula-hoop dancer.

"Out of my league. Over my head. The usual."

The high-strung studio assistant, Janet, who hummed about frantically but did nothing apparent, waved hello and pecked the screen of her smartphone purposefully.

Jo Ann covered an entire bench with her sculptures.

"What you got going on?" Luz loved asking Jo Ann about her sculptures because she blushed and stuttered when she had to explain her work. Even in high school, Jo Ann worked within the vagina motif. A little too O'Keeffe for Luz, but unlike Luz, Jo Ann actually made a living selling art.

"This," Jo Ann held up a slender curve of clay, "is a peace lily. Part of the seed."

Luz painted yellow into the young queen's bouffant wig.

"Who's that?" Jo Ann asked.

Luz heard insult in this question. Luz worked in miniature, so what? He made film instead of massive labias, so what? Normally he brought multiple sets and filled the kiln with his tiny world. What did Jo Ann care if progress was slow? "I'm spinning my wheels."

Jo Ann pointed to Mitzy. "I don't get it. Where is Anamosa? Where are you?"

Luz picked up one of the mock-ups for the neighbor's head. It was all wrong, lifeless, generic. Mitzy was no better; she could be any queen at any club. Luz turned the neighbor's face towards Jo Ann. "He loved her."

"No, honey. George offers you free rent and a studio and you bring in—who are these people—two months before the opening."

"Doesn't matter now," Luz said. "George and I are on the rocks."

"Like you're going to lose the condo?"

Luz shrugged.

"Get it together, Luz. Iowa. *He loved her,* you say. You want a romance, okay? What does Luz love?"

"What does it matter? Iowa isn't about love. Iowa is origins."

"Shut up. You have to tell me. Now. What is the origin story of Luz?"

"Changing the oil in my father's truck. Smoking with you behind Big Wheel. Blowing Kyle Richards in your mom's car.

Helping Mother mix biscuits. My sisters and I all in the same room whispering before sleep."

"Isn't that enough?"

"It wasn't. Why should it be now? Digging into all that makes me feel bad, like, I don't have a right to it anymore. Not since leaving, ignoring them for so long. All I have is love for a childhood I can't seem to see through my judgments as an adult. They hate fags and women and art and reading and they love God and money."

"Ain't that the truth. When I talked to my mom the other day, she told me that her church had prayed for a Republican victory, and when the last one won, she said if our new president is not enough of a reason to believe in God then nothing will save my soul."

"You talked to her this week?"

"Luz, seriously. You think my mom would go a week without calling me?"

Luz thought of George in that moment; the mind fantastically agile when dealing with thoughts of Mother; she thought of the many months that had passed since anyone from the family had called. George was persistent and Luz liked his begging; Luz was thirty years old and wanted stability so that he could dedicate more energy to art. The fact that financial and emotional stability rarely coincide, after all, didn't deter Luz from hoping the relationship might find a balance.

Luz didn't feel love from George.

Straight his whole life, married twice with two children, George only started calling himself queer the moment Luz moved into his condo, as if he'd not only acquired a hot, young thing, but also a hip new identity. He changed his Twitter and Facebook page to say Queer/Writer. Even though he *did* ask to be the bottom most nights, Luz resented this immediate co-opting of a life that had been a struggle since adolescence: queerness had forced Luz to search for other queers and had led him far from home, from Iowa and the chance of weekly parental phone calls. George couldn't just pick up a rainbow flag and march in line with everyone else who had fought before him, could he?

"All I'm saying is you might want to focus on yourself some," Jo Ann said. "Iowa was a much better plan and not without therapeutic value."

"You think I'm nuts?"

"I think you are very good at ignoring yourself."

That Friday night George made eggplant lasagna for dinner. He and Luz sat at the kitchen table, a gaudy glass-topped deal with brass legs from George's old life—the married life—like everything else in the apartment. George poured a glass of Pinot Noir for them both and hummed under his breath.

"Out with it. What's the good news?"

"Good news?" he said, fishing. "You're my lover."

Luz tilted the glass out to be refilled, made *come on now* eyes.

"*Bastion Hill* is going international," he said. "Mexico, Germany, England, and Canada. We're moving to Los Angeles!"

Luz sipped the wine. "Matter of time before something came of all the fuss, I guess."

"All the fuss?"

"Yeah. The fuss. *Bastion Hill* gets a lot of fuss."

"Listen," George said, "just celebrate with me."

"I'm celebrating." Luz downed the glass of wine and said, "See. I'm partying."

George frowned and poured. A pan of steaming lasagna sat on the table next to a salad with almonds and dried cranberries, Luz's favorite. Wearing a blue-and-orange polka-dotted apron, George fixed each plate. Luz cut a bite of cheese and eggplant, blowing to cool it. George remained standing.

"Stop hovering," Luz said.

"Wait. Put down your food." George wrestled his stubby fingers into his pocket and knelt at Luz's feet. He held out a black box, and as if proposing were as simple as dropping a lump of lasagna onto Luz's plate, George said, "Let's get married."

"No." Just like that. It was easy.

When the two finally went to bed after hours of fighting, breaking up, yelling the nuances of Luz's removal or George's refusal to return, after fucking and finally crashing naked and swollen atop the covers, Luz couldn't sleep. He felt crowded on the king mattress, mouth dry from too much wine and hours of crying. At 3 a.m., Luz heard pinched female vocals with violin. The music sounded far away but everywhere at the same time. He peered across the alley into the bright cinema of the neighbor's life who was dancing in a blue cotton robe, stepping back one-two then forward one-two.

Luz crawled from bed and pulled on sweatpants and a T-shirt.

He walked around back of the building. No light reached between the alley, and the ground blended as a textured mass. When Luz reached the complex, he looked up to George's apartment and sought out the tall studio windows and the lumpy silhouettes of marionettes. Wally was there, and Luz. Mitzy and the neighbor were half-finished on the workbench.

On the second floor, Luz heard music playing from behind the neighbor's door. He knocked. After a pause, the neighbor opened and stared back without speaking. He was much taller up close and his thin arms were sinewy with muscle.

"Can I help you?"

Luz recognized the music. A waltz he remembered from dance classes in Anamosa.

"I'm sorry. I—"

The neighbor studied Luz. "I recognize you," he whispered and pointed to the windows that faced George's condo. He made a wide expression with his eyes that said *I recognize all of you*.

"I guess that's why I'm here—"

"Uh-uh. You put some blinds up," the neighbor said, raising his voice.

"I wanted to meet you. Talk with you—"

TV applause erupted from the apartment behind them and the neighbor's eyes flicked in the direction of the sound. Someone coughed and snorted deep.

"You got to move on," he said, pointing to the door across the hall. "If the manager finds you here, I'm out on the street. Don't you know this place is a halfway house? We're not allowed visitors. So go before he catches us."

Luz saw that he meant to turn away. "I've been watching you." Luz looked past the neighbor and into the living room, towards the crate set up in front of his window with taffeta over the top, candles burning low. A boa was tacked like a coiled snake on the window frame above the shrine; flames licked the bottom feathers causing them to curl. Mitzy. Something rose up inside Luz, rose up into his abdomen, all blood and muscle.

"What do you want from me?"

"Where is she? The drag queen in your shrine?"

"I'm going to close this door. Take your ass back across the way, and stay out of my business."

From the manager's room, a bottle dropped and rolled across hardwood, empty by the sound of it but a clear sign of danger—a screech of springs, footsteps dooming. Wax sizzled inside the neighbor's room.

"Let me inside." All bravado had vanished and Luz's voice sounded soft. The neighbor would not talk, would not let Luz any nearer to his life than the threshold of his front door.

"Go home, honey. Wherever that is, just go." The neighbor closed his door.

Not wanting to sneak down the alley, Luz chose the main stairs. He left through the front door, as if he too had been living in this halfway house and was now free to go. He walked past George's condo and toward the Basilica. Jo Ann would be asleep, but would wake up when Luz knocked. She would make him a bed of the sofa and let him borrow her truck in the morning to move his things into storage. Home, the neighbor said, "wherever that is." It was not Iowa, but it was not with George either. When he reached the three-way intersection, Luz noticed that the traffic signal had been fixed. The light changed from red to green, drawing long shadows across the pavement. Luz stopped at the corner and watched the cycle twice: Green. Yellow. Red. Green. Go. Yellow. Slow. Red—No cars came, no other people either. No one but Luz witnessed the lights change.

ACKNOWLEDGMENTS

I would like to thank the late Katherine Min for her guidance, humor, and friendship.

The stories in this collection have passed through many compassionate and willful readers along the way. I am so grateful to have Grant Gerald Miller and Mesha Maren in my life, both as lifelong friends and fellow artists.

I would like to thank Daniel Wallace, Ashleigh Bryant Phillips, JP Gritton, and Juliet Escoria for their kind blurbs.

The incredibly talented staff at Autumn House deserves great recognition for the work they put into running a small press with such sincerity and dedication. Christine Stroud is an impeccable editor that wears many hats and I am so grateful to have worked with her. I'd also like to thank Mike Good, Shelby Newsom, and Kinsley Stocum.

Most of these stories have been published in journals and magazines. Thank you to Aaron Burch and Elizabeth Ellen at *Hobart* for publishing "Heads Down" in *Hobart* #13. Thank you to Robert Stapleton for publishing "Shadow Play" in issue # 7 of *Booth*. Thank you to Barry Kitterman and the staff at *Zone 3* for publishing and awarding "Hallelujah Station" a *Zone 3* Literary Award. Thanks to the staff at *QU* for publishing "Rembrandt Behind Windows." Thank you, *The Masters Review* for publishing "Luz" (née "Luces").

New and Forthcoming Releases

under the aegis of a winged mind by makalani bandele ♦
Winner of the 2019 Autumn House Poetry Prize, selected by
Cornelius Eady

Hallelujah Station and Other Stories by M. Randal O'Wain

Grimoire by Cherene Sherrard

Further News of Defeat: Stories by Michael X. Wang ♦ Winner of
the 2019 Autumn House Fiction Prize, selected by Aimee Bender

Skull Cathedral: A Vestigial Anatomy by Melissa Wiley ♦ Winner
of the 2019 Autumn House Nonfiction Prize, selected by Paul
Lisicky

No One Leaves the World Unhurt by John Foy ♦ Winner of the
2020 Donald Justice Prize, selected by J. Allyn Rosser

In the Antarctic Circle by Dennis James Sweeney ♦ Winner of the
2020 Autumn House Rising Writer Prize, selected by Yona Harvey

Creep Love by Michael Walsh

The Dream Women Called by Lori Wilson

For our full catalog please visit: http://www.autumnhouse.org